WOMEN OF WHITE EARTH

Photographs and Interviews by Vance Vannote
With editorial assistance from Janet Pratt

WOMEN

University of Minnesota Press — Minneapolis — London

OF WHITE EARTH

Copyright 1999 by the Regents of the University of Minnesota

All rights reserved. No part of this publication may be reproduced, stored in a retrieval system, or transmitted, in any form or by any means, electronic, mechanical, photocopying, recording, or otherwise, without the prior written permission of the publisher.

Published by the University of Minnesota Press
111 Third Avenue South, Suite 290
Minneapolis, MN 55401-2520
http://www.upress.umn.edu

Library of Congress Cataloging-in-Publication Data

Vannote, Vance.
    Women of white earth / photographs and interviews by Vance Vannote, with editorial assistance from Janet Pratt.
      p.   cm.
    ISBN 0-8166-3274-X (pbk.)
    1. Ojibwa women—Minnesota—White Earth Indian Reservation Interviews. 2. Ojibwa women—Minnesota—White Earth Indian Reservation Portraits. I. Pratt, Janet, 1935– . II. Title.
E99.C6V37   1999
305.48′8973077694—dc21   99-42686

Printed in the United States of America on acid-free paper

The University of Minnesota is an equal-opportunity educator and employer.

11 10 09 08 07 06 05 04 03 02 01 00 99   10 9 8 7 6 5 4 3 2 1

For Michele and all of my family

Contents

Preface　ix

Acknowledgments　xiii

Kimberly Blaeser　3

Gladys Ray　8

Yvonne Novack　13

Diana Osborn-King　18

Dena Rae Iron Cloud　23

Kathleen Renee Annette　27

Lorna Jean LaGue　33

Theresa Olsen　38

Blanche Turner　43

Leah Carpenter　47

Thelma Wang　52

Mary Harper　57

Ronda Sargent-Estey　63

Valerie Fox　68

Saraphine Martin　73

Juanita Blackhawk	77
Lorraine Faye Lindsay	82
Angelique Marie Stevens	87
Erma Vizenor	92
Janet Sara Gordon-Roy	97
Lena Desizlets	102
Sue Bellefeuille	107
Anita Fineday	112
Ann LaVoy	117
Anne M. Dunn	122
Bonnie Faye Wadena	127
Marcie Rendon	131
Delores Rousu	136
Irene Auginaush-Turney	141
Joan Staples	146
Verna Millage	151
Eleanore Robertson	156
Natalie Ann Greenlaw	161
Winona LaDuke	166
Marilyn Thelen	170
Myrna Joyce Smith	175
Michelle Lea Bellanger-Azure	179
Melody LaFriniere	183
Ellen (Ellie Mae) Robinson	188
Elizabeth Foster-Anderson	193
Leigh Harper	198
Beverly Warren	202
Frances Keahna	207

Preface

In 1993 I experienced Brian Lanker's wonderful exhibit of the vivid, unforgettable images and words of influential black women in America. The richly textured photographs and timely interviews he produced, both in his exhibit and book, were the inspiration for my efforts in this project, which I began in early 1994.

Photography and the emotional impact of visual images have been lifelong interests of mine, and as I thought of how I might employ the portrait-and-interview approach, I considered various regional populations as possibilities. After discussions with several members of the White Earth Reservation community, I decided to present a contemporary perspective of women enrolled in the White Earth Reservation.

The history of the White Earth Reservation is unique, complex, and varied. The fabric of the reservation is woven from the material of so many sources that it almost defies a unified description or interpretation. But even more unique, complex, and varied are the women who today are tribal members of White Earth. It has been my privilege through this work to meet and know a small number of them, and these associations have forever altered my previous perceptions. My hope is that this work may have a similar impact on the reader and that, in addition, the personal observations and comments of the women about the history and function of the reservation itself will prove enlightening and informative.

It appears to me that almost every woman I photographed and interviewed has faced and struggled with adversity in some form—and has survived through an inherent strength and courage. Other than this similarity, and the fact that these individuals are all women and enrolled members, there is no convenient, facile way to categorize these women. There are some similarities, to be sure, but their personalities, life histories, thoughts, and points of view are as different as the visual images of their portraits.

The significance of their Indian heritage varied from woman to woman. For some it has been life defining and of critical importance; for others it has been a fact to be reckoned with but no more meaningful than other influences. I believe I have presented these women in a positive light not only by recording their successes but also by showing their strength, spirit, and continuing perseverance in facing past and current hardships and adversity. Like their culture and society, these women continue to evolve and change in dynamic ways. Their images and words are a moment in time in their lives, recorded on the dates each woman was photographed and interviewed. They have moved on and will continue to move on. By now some will have experienced notable changes in their circumstances. Some will have switched jobs; others will have retired. Some will have moved away; others will have moved back. Perhaps some will have modified or even reversed their expressed opinions. Some will have continued their education; others will have graduated. And for at least one, Frances Keahna, the final change of crossing over to the other side has been made.

These changes reflect a basic premise of the work: these women are not a static collective but are individuals with dreams, goals, failures, accomplishments, and ambitions. They are influenced and molded by personal histories, cultural heritage, family values, religious and spiritual beliefs, sexual identity, professional and work experience, educational exposure, and political events. They are homemakers, caregivers, professionals, traditionalists, activists, leaders, and urban and rural grandmothers, mothers, daughters, artists, craftswomen, and students. Some were born on and some were born off the reservation; some live on the reservation now, and others do not. All are enrolled as members of the White Earth Reservation.

A brief explanation about the process and methods used in collecting the information in this book, and also about how this information was distilled and edited into its final form, is appropriate. All of the interviews (except one) were conducted before the photographs were taken. Each woman was interviewed by the author in a face-to-face tape-recorded meeting that lasted between one and three hours. These interviews were wide-ranging and open-ended discussions prompted by questions from the author. The recorded interviews were transcribed, and the difficult process of editing then began. Editing down to an average of seventeen hundred words what were often freewheeling conversations covering from thirty to sixty typewritten pages is a daunting task, and primary among the many decisions that had to be made were what to include and what to cut. The women had so much to say that was relevant and of great interest, yet literary justice often could not be done to their interviews considering how much had to be excluded. The goal was not to obtain a complete biography of each woman's life, however, but to provide a sample of their thoughts and words to enhance the visual image of their portraits, to give the reader a glimpse of various aspects of the women's lives and their perceptions of the world around them. Much of the material is comprised of direct quotations, but rather than a verbatim report this is an edited version constructed to enhance readability. The author's questions were deleted, transitions between topics were clarified, material was reordered to promote the flow of thought, and other editorial functions were performed. I hope the meaning of the thoughts and the voices of the women, in addition to their visual images, are reflected on the following pages.

Acknowledgments

When I initially conceived of this book several years ago, it never occurred to me that it would take as long as it has to complete, and, frankly, there were times when I questioned the wisdom of continuing. Since I began, it has been a labor of love—a love of the emotional impact of visual images and of the complexity of the human spirit. I have spent hundreds of hours in the darkroom, on the telephone, in front of the computer, conducting interviews, taking photographs, traveling and lugging camera equipment to the reservation and other locations, reviewing the transcripts and manuscript, and discussing the work with editors. Tempted though I am to claim ownership as a result of my efforts, I know this book is a collective endeavor of many who have helped and encouraged me along the way; it would not have been possible without them.

Obviously, without the acceptance and participation of the women of the Anishinabe people the project would not have gotten off the ground. They warmly and graciously welcomed me into their homes and offices, and on occasion they even came to my home to be interviewed. They agreed to sit for portraits and were patient with the time-consuming process of photography despite their own busy schedules. They introduced me to family members; fed me cake, cookies, and pie; and gave me gifts of poetry and blankets. Best of all, they shared with me their thoughts and feelings in an open and trusting manner.

The search for editors to review and condense the hundreds of pages of transcript from the recorded interviews led to my friendship with three wonderful women. Nancy Edmonds-Hanson helped formulate the proposal for the book and edited the initial transcripts submitted to the publisher; thanks in part to her efforts, the project was accepted for publication. Just as important as her expertise were Nancy's personal support and encouragement. When time restraints and her own work schedule prevented Nancy from continuing, Elizabeth Peterson stepped in; her insight and observations, along with her sense of humor, were most welcome. Finally, Janet Pratt took charge of the overall editing process, and because of her belief in the project and her respect for Anishinabe women, she did a tremendous amount of work. This book exists because of Janet's involvement and her ability to condense the interviews and still maintain the authenticity of the women's voices and the integrity of their stories.

Doyle Turner and his wife, Mary, listened to my ideas and lent their support, which was critical in the initial stages. They also provided a list of names for me to contact and acted as intermediaries, which gave the project and my efforts credibility. Don Doll, S.J., professor at Creighton University, where he holds the Charles and Mary Heider Jesuit Chair, was kind enough to review my work and offer his support to the project.

Erma Vizenor was one of the first people with whom I spoke when considering this idea. She was very encouraging, as were many others, including Kimberly Blaeser, who first mentioned it to the editors at the University of Minnesota Press. Todd Orjala, Jennifer Moore, Laura Westlund, and Amy Unger of the Press all provided much-needed advice and guidance throughout the publication process.

Colleen Eck capably and dependably transcribed and typed the many hours of recorded interviews for editing and also offered her suggestions. Kelly Pratt-Raymond helped straighten out the computer messes that I created more than once. Many others helped in ways too numerous and diverse to mention; these include James and Sue Murray, Sally and David Suby, Gale Gish, Tom Williams, Sandy Gronhovd, Robert Washnieski, Brad Bremer, Carreen Pierson, Yvonne Mulry, Paul Gaffaney, Jane Gudmundson, Wayne Gudmundson, Erin Conroy, Kathy Borge, The MarketPlace, LLC, and Nick Blade.

Perhaps most important, special thanks to my good friend John Borge. John is an accomplished photographer with an abundance of energy who, in spite of his busy schedule, shared with me his expertise and knowledge. He let me use his finely equipped studios and facilities and often went out of his way to provide guidance, constructive criticism, and suggestions—always in the positive manner of a good teacher encouraging self-confidence and growth in a willing student.

I have always drawn on the strength of my family, and this journey was no exception. In addition, the extended clan of in-laws, nephews and nieces, and even young grandchildren probably heard much more about photography and this project than they ever wanted to, but they listened patiently anyway.

And last, of course, is Michele. There is always Michele!

WOMEN OF WHITE EARTH

Kimberly Blaeser lives in Burlington, Wisconsin, with her husband, Lenny. She grew up in the Mahnomen, Minnesota, area and in Billings, Montana. A graduate of Mahnomen High School, she earned her undergraduate degree at the College of St. Benedict in St. Joseph, Minnesota, and her master's and doctorate in English from the University of Notre Dame in 1982 and 1990, respectively. In 1987 she joined the faculty of the University of Wisconsin-Milwaukee. She has written both popular and scholarly articles for a variety of journals and magazines. Her recent book, a collection of poetry titled *Trailing You,* draws heavily on her youthful experiences on the White Earth Indian Reservation.

Kimberly Blaeser
Born: August 31, 1958

When I was growing up, I didn't know we were poor. I didn't know that we sometimes did not have a lot of money for food. I was sheltered—as children are—by the comfort of family and its playfulness, joys, and closeness. That makes you feel rich as a child. My older brother, Robert, and I were the center of our parents' world. They devoted their time to making us happy, and we enjoyed each other. We had such good times.

My dad is German and my mom is Indian; her family is part of the Mississippi band of the White Earth Tribe. She grew up around Nay-tah-waush and on a farm near Beaulieu, Minnesota. Our family was the typical kind of Indian family. It included my grandpa and grandma, aunts and uncles, and lots of cousins.

I suppose I had a strange childhood in a way, at least according to what was typical in the big world, the white world. We lived in many different places—not in the sense of being a transient, but really feeling at home. We spent summers in Montana, where my dad worked on construction part of the year. But we also spent a lot of time on the farm with my grandma and grandpa, where lots of other people might be staying at different times, or we spent time with relatives in Nay-tah-waush or Twin Lakes. It wasn't a big deal. We really did feel at home in all these places. For example, no one knocked on doors; you just went on in, because that was your home too in a way.

By the time I was ready for kindergarten, we were living in Mahnomen, Minnesota, most of the year in a house my dad owned on Main Street. We tried living in Billings for one school year, but we ended up coming home after only one semester. I think my mom got too homesick, so we just came back. My dad would get home by Christmas and then leave us again in the spring. When school was out, we'd take the train to Billings to meet him. That went on for four or five years. I remember the pattern so well. I have so many memories attached even to that train ride.

I was very attached to my dad, and missed him terribly when we were alone in Mahnomen. I remember longing for him while he was gone. When I was starting kindergarten, I'd always have earaches—or maybe I just was lonesome for him and didn't really have the earaches. When I was really sad, I'd go into the closet where some of his clothes were kept just to smell them and get a sense of his presence.

My mother spent hours and hours making little school exercises, and we'd play school. She and my other relatives read to us all the time. My father recited poetry. I think my relatives, especially my parents, gave us a real sense of story. Reading and stories have always been really important to our family. We were given the sense of being responsible for ourselves, of knowing what was good and what wasn't. They did it by telling us stories. We may never have met the people in some of the stories, but they're part of our family history, and the stories have a moral [within them]—not stated, but shown through what someone did. Indian people don't *teach* their children. They *story* them.

My parents rewarded us by appreciating us and being proud of what we did in school. They were truly happy with what we accomplished. Somehow that made us want to do well. I still feel strongly that, for the sake of my parents and my relatives, I would like to accomplish what they didn't have a chance to try. They created me, and I am they. They've supported me, in the past and today, in a way that's very unselfish. That's not the way the rest of the world operates. I feel a strong sense of commitment to them.

When I look at my relatives, I see good people. I admire so many of them. My mom instilled that sense of admiration for her father and mother, her grandparents, my aunts and uncles, and especially for older people. Indian people are joyous people, but I think there might be a sadness or hollowness inside of them. In some ways, my parents had a very hard life, and I'm sad about that. In earlier times, it was difficult, at best, for Indian and non-Indian people to be together.

I feel the need to write about certain things that have happened in my life because it's cathartic, or healing in some way or a way to put it in order. I try to have whatever I write feel true, whether or not I choose to include all the details that might interest people. I think very carefully about what to present. I could spend a lot of time vividly re-creating things that do people very little good. I don't feel right now that I have a need to let the world know about those things. That's not to say I'll never write about them. But it seems to me that part of what I do as a writer is healing other people as well as myself. Somehow it's a gift.

A friend once told me, "Indian people can hold more than one thing sacred." That's how I feel. I was raised Catholic, with all its traditions and beliefs. At the same time, I believe the natural world is as significant as we are, while the Bible tells us that man has dominion over the creatures of the earth. I hold many of the Indian teachings very sacred—and many Christian teachings as well.

It's a balancing act—but, then, my whole life is a balancing act. I've always been on the border. I'm a mixed-blood, I'm educated, and I lived on the res. There are countless ways in which I'm always crossing and recrossing those borders.

To me, being able to keep a spiritual balance means believing in things that are good without having to swallow whole any one philosophy. I think that some parts of us come from our ancestors, come in our blood. We could call it "intuition." Maybe we develop it the moment we are born. How do we know things about the world? About its power?

My husband doesn't have the same fear of authority that I do. I feel that I'm a part of the Indian community—and the world is the white community. I've always had the feeling of being an alien, as if there were rules and barriers that made things inaccessible. But growing up, I didn't have an identity crisis about being Indian. In a small community, everyone knows you and your family and where you come from: You're Indian. In Indian communities, people welcome you. They recognize you. They don't question your identity.

That's not always clear in the outside world. In high school, I remember taking a bus to a speech contest with my English teacher. The gentleman in front of us knew we were from White Earth. As people often are, he was very inquisitive and asked a lot of questions. I felt very angry because I thought he was being insensitive. My teacher finally said, "Oh, are you interested in Indians? Kim is Indian." He turned purple; he'd been saying things that you would not say to a Native American. His instinctive reaction was, "Oh, you have lovely cheekbones."

I have written about a past encounter with a professor's wife. She looked at me doubtfully and said, "But Indians don't have curly hair." I told her, "I don't have curly hair either. It's a perm."

It wasn't cool to be an Indian when I was growing up, not in Mahnomen. Certain things were kept secret in my family. If someone came to the house, for instance, and we were having venison for dinner, my mother would say, "It's chicken." My parents would take us out of school to go fishing or to some Indian cultural event, but they'd make up stories. It was clearly established in my mind that these worlds were supposed to be kept separate.

That remains true for me. My perspective shifts almost the moment I return to this place [White Earth]. I think it's very good for me now. When my husband and I were dating, he'd call me up here, but he wouldn't recognize my voice because I had switched into a reservation accent. For a long time, he'd be confused and think he was talking to my mom. I think now I have a voice that sort of goes with me wherever I am—but maybe not completely.

I think that feeling of crossing borders has an effect on my poetry, too. I write in all sorts of genres, and don't really see the distinctions that are set up by our academic system. Some of my poetry is very narrative, very much like a story. I've written some pieces that physically cross over: They may look like poetry at one point and like prose at another. I try to make the sound of the human voice come across in everything I write. I have all these voices living inside me, all these people—what they've said or haven't been able to say.

The last time I was home, I did a reading in Bemidji. My Aunt Blanche came, along with her daughter and two of her granddaughters, a cousin, her son, and his fiancée. I had never actually read to members of my family before. It was both nerve-wracking and also such a good feeling, because they knew these stories, these people, these places I write about. To have them appreciate and enjoy what I've written and to have it mean something to them—that meant to me that in some special way I had succeeded. When I think about the audiences for my work, the most important for me are the Indian people. They know whether it's real.

Gladys Ray

Born: January 3, 1933

Gladys Ray is looking back on her life and realizing that many of the things she accomplished were because she was at the right place at the right time. She has been instrumental in various community economic opportunity programs. She has learned a great deal from the volunteers she worked with in her numerous pursuits. One particular program she remembers is Project Bridge, an organization meant to create understanding between the Indian and the non-Indian communities. She was named Woman of the Year in 1973 by the Fargo-Moorhead YWCA for her work in furthering understanding between the two cultures.

My grandparents moved from a Wisconsin border town to White Earth to claim their land allotment. This area was being set up as Indian country. I suspect this was a move by the government to destroy the Indian culture and to break up the various societies. I believe the government built my family's first house there; but when that house burned, my grandfather built a two-story log house. That's where I was born.

My grandparents practiced a way of life called *Midewiwin.* Our whole family was brought up in the Midewiwin ways, but we were one of the few families on the reservation that still followed this way of life. I think the main reason I have stayed with my own culture and religion is because of my grandparents. I respected them. They were such a large part of my childhood. I was very fond of these beautiful old people. I've always felt that if I could be the kind of grandma that my grandma was to me, then I really had succeeded in my life. My grandma and grandpa had time for us. They were our teachers and counselors, a constant reminder of who we were—who I was.

I saw a lot of prejudice and discrimination long before I came to the city. I was in the eighth grade in Mahnomen when I read that the Indians were pagans. I became very angry and told the teacher, "This is not a true statement." To me this was directed at my own grandparents, who practiced their way of life every day. They didn't swear like I heard other people doing, and they never treated anyone badly. When I would ask, "Grandpa, why do the kids tease me and why are they so mean?," he would say, "Oh, that's all right, my girl. They don't know what they are doing." It helped me to deal with things all the rest of my life—just a few simple words. That's how they lived their lives. How could they be bad people?

My parents believed in education, but often we had difficulty even getting to school. My dad went to see the principal at Mahnomen one day to report trouble with the bus. The principal refused to deal with us. He told my dad, "Well, Mr. Shingobe, if you don't like the way we do things here, just throw in the towel." This meant that we should just quit school.

My brother decided to "throw in the towel." I continued. I found a job at a place where the bus drove by every day; there was no way they could skip over me now. So I finished eighth grade that way. By the end of the year, I was able to pass the state boards. Then I went to Indian School and graduated in 1951. I liked the Indian School. You could get out of it what you wanted. The information was there to be learned. It was up to you. I wasn't the most brilliant child in the world, but I put a lot of effort into it and made honor roll most of the time.

After I finished school, I enlisted and served two years in the Women's Army Corps. This was interesting for me because I discovered that it wasn't hard for me to compete with people of all colors. Being Indian put me in the middle sometimes. I wasn't black and I wasn't white. I think that's why they sent me to leadership training and then put me somewhere in the middle of the barracks so I could help keep order.

I've always been sure of who I am spiritually. As a child, I had gained enough understanding of this to carry me through. This helped me when we moved to Fargo. My husband was white, and we didn't know anyone, let alone any other Indian people. But in time, we made lots of friends.

Most of my family stayed on the reservation or nearby, and we go back sometimes. And we have our graves there. The burial grounds became a problem that surfaced in 1942, when my grandfather died. There were new laws. The organized churches didn't want "pagans" buried in their cemeteries. It looked like my grandfather couldn't get buried in his own country. Then my father had some land designated as an Indian cemetery so we could bury my grandfather. My grandmother and my mother are now buried there, too.

I have really spent my life doing work for our people. I feel sometimes that my destiny has been directed. It started in 1960, when I was asked to be a speaker on a panel for the Fargo-Moorhead YWCA. I learned a lot of shocking statistics as I was reading and preparing for this panel. I felt that as a human being, even with only a twelfth-grade education, I ought to be able to do something to help change things.

One thing led to another. I've worked for Community Action Agency programs and other economic opportunity programs. I was asked to go to Denver for the Model Cities Program. I learned so much about government agencies. I served at the state, regional, and national level for Community Action Agency programs and the Office of Economic Opportunity.

One time I was hired to do a survey of Indian people in our community. As a result of the survey, we organized the Indian Club and the Indian Center. A lot of interest was beginning to surface in the community and in the nation. For example, during the 1970s, the American Indian Movement was doing a lot to shake things up and sensitize people. Many churches became interested, too. About this time, I was asked to be on a panel for the "Communiversity" at Concordia College. I was in the right place at the right time. I was scared to death. I don't remember what I talked about, but we got an offer of a building for an Indian Center—a beautiful old building, standing vacant, that we could use. We didn't have any money, but I became the coordinator. I started with minimum wage.

I made many non-Indian friends during this time, people who were very influential in the community. A result of this was Project Bridge, an organization meant to build bridges between the Indian and the non-Indian communities. Through Project Bridge, we were able to do a lot of things. We started with critiques of history texts in the Fargo public schools. Social workers, educators, lawyers, professors, all kinds of people helped with this project. It was a monumental task! Doing the critiques, I learned why I hated history. But the people I worked with were always very supportive of what we were trying to accomplish.

During the years I worked on all these committees and projects, I was also raising a family. My husband and I had six children. Of course, they are half-Indian, but I think I started too late to work with them on their attitudes about their heritage. The children were influenced by what they learned in school. I have a funny story to illustrate this. When I first took my children back to the reservation, they were all very young and close together in age. One day my husband and I took four of the children back to visit an elder whom I had known all my life. The kids were squabbling over who got to sit by the window. When we got near the reservation, I said, "Well, we're in Indian country now, my old stomping grounds." I was kidding around, but the kids got awfully quiet. One of the kids spoke up and said, "Dad, the Indians don't come out 'til night, do they? By that time we'll be home, won't we, Dad?" Our son was scared of Indians, and he was only three. It struck me as funny, humorous that they should be afraid of Indians. They don't see themselves as Indians. My parents were always around, but the children never considered them Indians either. The Indians they were hearing about were hostile.

I know people who still walk the Indian way. They live in the community and go on about their lives. And there are those who still practice the rituals in their everyday lives. The medicine people, the pipe carriers, the drummers carry ideas and beliefs that belong to the native people, and I think they should be kept there. I don't see any need to incorporate the Native American spirituality into the churches. There is definitely a line that separates the things that are spiritual from the material. I think we need to respect that line in our religions and beliefs.

I said at the beginning that I had one foot in each of two different worlds. I've raised a family in a white community, I was involved in my community in many ways, and I held a job at the Veterans Administration for a while. I've enjoyed it all, and I've learned a lot. But I was raised the Indian way, and I still have that identity. I've made lots of friends, and I was even recognized for my work. In 1973 the Fargo-Moorhead YWCA honored me with the Woman of the Year award in the volunteer category. I also received the Service to Mankind award from Sertoma and an award from the Hjemkomst Center. I was shocked; I couldn't believe it. There are so many people who have done so many things. I think I was selected because no one had ever done Indian work. It wasn't because I had done anything so great.

I am glad I have a lot of things to do since my husband died of cancer. My life has never really settled down. I'm working on a rice project now, and people at White Earth are asking me to help teach some of our cultural things. I am involved in ceremonies both here and in White Earth. My life is very full. There is wealth in our culture, and my people are rich in many ways. But there is a lot of work yet to be done.

Yvonne Novack is the director of Indian education in Minnesota, coordinating and overseeing all the state programs in this area. She is the oldest daughter in a family of eight children. Her mother came from the White Earth Reservation. Her father was white and held a master's degree in fine arts; he was a civilian employee for the Army whose job caused the family to move several times. The children attended many different schools, but they settled in the San Jose area after the eighth child was born. Yvonne's grandfather John L. Pemberton enrolled all his grandchildren at White Earth, which Yvonne has always considered her home. She graduated from Berkeley in 1987, and received a master's degree in education from Harvard. She is interested in systemic changes in education that will better meet the needs of individual children of all races.

Yvonne Novack
Born: June 22, 1949

I think I'm in education today because of my mother's negative experiences in school. She was determined that her kids would have educational opportunities that she had not had. We kids went to private and Catholic schools in Indianapolis and Chicago; we finally settled in California, when I was about ten or eleven. Traveling all over, we learned that people have different stereotypical pictures of what an Indian is. We kids always knew we were Indian. Sometimes people would ask if my mother was Italian because she is darker than I am. I would say, "No, she's Indian." They would reply, "Indians are dead." When kids would ask us what we Indians did for Thanksgiving, our line was that we would invite some Pilgrims to dinner. We learned a lot living all over the United States.

My mother passed on to us information and understanding about our heritage. Somehow we knew who we were. We knew who our grandfather was. He was prominent in Indian politics until his death in 1962. He and other family members would visit us from time to time. I believe that even if you are in a different setting from where you grew up, certain values and traditions are passed on to the children. I know definitely that my mom gave us something that kept us tied to White Earth.

I graduated from Berkeley in 1987 with a degree in Native American studies. I realized by that point that I was an educator. I was especially interested in how Indian kids face things in school. During my previous nine years of working in a public high school system, it became clear that when kids aren't validated, problems start—academically, socially, and every way. This is especially important for Indian kids who know they're Indian with strong tribal backgrounds but who have only seen movie and TV stereotypes about what an Indian is. In urban Indian populations, this sense of identity means so much. But these kids were far from their reservations; they couldn't go home, and they deserved a safe and welcoming environment in school. Most of them weren't getting this.

By the time I graduated from Berkeley, I had applied for a job to be a principal at a small school in the middle-of-nowhere, Nevada. I had also applied and been accepted to Harvard Graduate School, but I didn't think I could go because it would be such a financial struggle. My stepfather and son helped me to decide to try it. "If you don't do it now, you never will," my stepfather said. This advice, plus the fact that I had always dreamed of ending up back in Minnesota, helped me decide. I went to Harvard and spent a year in the master's program in education. The concentration of the work was administration planning and social policy.

While I was there, I began wondering, "How do you make changes in public schools? How do you change state bureaucracy?" While I was asking these questions, I was selected as a Woodrow Wilson Administrative Fellow. I was the first Indian woman ever to be chosen for that. After that, I worked as the director of instructional services at Fond du Lac Community College in Cloquet, Minnesota. From there I went to a job as the deputy administrator of the Center of American Indian and Minority Health at the University of Minnesota-Duluth. This required some experience I didn't have. I had to manage a ten-million-dollar budget and work at the graduate level. All this time, I was learning by experience and meeting people who were really looking at Indian education. This was when I met Ruth Meyers, who started encouraging me to apply for the job I have now. At first I told her I was very happy with the job I had, but then I began to realize that the past twenty years of experience and education had prepared me for this job, so I applied. I really wanted to make a difference, and I wanted to see kids stay in school and not drop out.

I also started to notice that racism in Minnesota is much more hidden than in other places I had lived. People don't want to discuss it or look at it, but it is there, along with a kind of moral condescension. It's hard to explain, but when you are an Indian woman who has been to Harvard and you have a son in the schools, people look at you and wonder why you look at things as an Indian. They don't understand that I look at things as an educator and that some things are unique for the Indian student.

My first year back was spent trying to make programs accountable. I believe this requires systemic change. I think that, after all these years, we are still sort of stuck in the middle. What I'm striving for is an equal education for Indian kids.

The Indians in this country are different from other minority groups because we have a government and a separate political entity. We didn't arrive in this country to escape anything. We were already here. Our culture and government were already established. The tribal governments have survived, even those that don't have designated reservations. I would like to see some real information about Indian history added to public schools' graduation requirements. When kids grow up and graduate, they need to know some facts before they can deal with issues like treaties, gaming, sovereignty, and so on. It's not enough for our kids to learn a little bit about the Hopis, the Navahos, and the Cherokees. That's fun to learn about, but we need to integrate some facts into the curriculum, just as we teach about the American government—federal, state, and local issues. It really comes down to mutual respect for each other's culture and history. When we have knowledge and understanding, we don't fear as much, and it's much easier to get along.

I think I've changed my mind about education in the past few years. I think we create our own cultural myths that perpetuate attitudes and don't help our kids. I believe that we educators need to look at these myths and see if they are valid or not. We need to open doors and take another look at what we believe to be true.

In the Ojibwe culture, people's individual voices are highly valued. Individuals with different perspectives can share a history that holds them together. I come from a very strong line of women. My great-grandmother and her family, for example, were removed to White Earth when my Grandmother Louise was about five years old. She had strong traditional beliefs, but she taught her kids what they needed to know to survive in the white world. I was brought back to meet my great-grandmother six months before she died. I got to know her through stories I've been told. My Grandmother Louise and her sister Lilian were sent to Carlisle Indian School when they were about eleven years old; they stayed until they were seventeen and never came home. They got business degrees after high school, but no one would hire them, so they came home to the res. They were strong women.

I think these women lost more than culture and language; they also lost the chance to practice parenting skills because they weren't living with a family. I wonder how my grandmother did it. It must have been very hard when she returned and raised thirteen kids.

Most of the boarding schools have disappeared now. There are probably about five across the United States. It's interesting that some of that generation do not have the animosity that the next generation has about being sent to boarding schools. It's like a delayed reaction.

My grandmother's stories about Carlisle often mention how she missed her family. But she did learn a lot of things, and she didn't have to experience poverty. Boarding schools are different experiences for different people because of what their parents were able to give them before they left. Not having good parental modeling, I have heard, was even harder on the boys who went to boarding school. What was left for these Indian men to do? Either work for the government or work seasonally doing different things or manage things that once had been theirs. At least in the Ojibwe culture, the women had a chance to return and continue their roles. They could be strong and still have a voice.

I was raised Roman Catholic. But many of the beliefs I hold today are tied to the Ojibwe beliefs. I don't practice Midewiwin, but I have attended ceremonies. I believe not everything is definable: there are things we cannot explain, and maybe those are spiritual things that don't fit into our own religious history. Some things that have happened to me have really opened me up to the Ojibwe spirituality and have become a reality for me. Personally I'm still growing and I'm still looking. I don't have a rigid way of looking at things. As you learn and grow, certain things make sense and others don't. It's all a process.

Diana Osborn-King
Born: June 28, 1949

Diana Osborn-King has strong feelings about her heritage and traditional beliefs. She considers herself an activist whose main interest is in helping her people. After graduating from college, she was instrumental in establishing Head Start programs and increasing the number of Native American children enrolled in the program. Her work has led her into the world of politics and advocacy. At the time of the interview, Diana was working to achieve equity for Indians in existing programs and to support the efforts of Senator Paul Wellstone of Minnesota.

My dad was a teacher who graduated from Bemidji State University on the GI Bill and moved us out to the West Coast, where we lived and traveled by foot with a lot of migrant workers. We lived along the Columbia River at a time when Indians could still net the river. We saw the progress of the salmon companies taking control of the river and the Indians' right to net being reduced and reduced until a time came when they couldn't fish the Columbia at all.

My mother had very strong Indian values. Her mother was the last one in our family to be brought up on the reservation. Grandmother had been taken away from her family the first time when she was four years old and put into a government boarding school. The second time she was taken away, she was eight or nine and put into a school at Pipestone, Minnesota. I still grieve for the pain my grandmother must have felt when she was taken away from her family. That's why I dance at Pipestone now. It's like a healing for me to remember this story. I walk along the hill in Pipestone and see all the graves of the Indian children who died there and were never returned to their people. I know that my grandmother could just as well have been in one of those small graves.

We came back to Minnesota when I was in the seventh grade. We lived in several different places and finally settled in Cass Lake. Then I became more aware of what my heritage was and who I was as a person. It was hard to define ourselves in large cities, where there were so many minorities, but in Cass Lake it was clear. There was a division—the railroad track: the Indians were on one side of the road and the white people on the other. There was a real need to stick together then.

When I was eighteen, I married an Indian boy. I probably would have been just a nice quiet girl, a homemaker, but my husband was killed at age nineteen in a car accident. I had a six-month-old baby, and I didn't know what to do. This changed my life.

When I got pregnant, my husband and I were living in Minneapolis right down near the Indian Center in a terrible place with cockroaches. We wanted a better, cleaner place to live. One day we saw a sign, "Apartment for Rent," on the front of a building where we thought people wouldn't be coming and going all night and we would feel more secure. We went in to inquire. The owner took one look at us and said, "I'm sorry, we don't rent to Indians." We walked back out to the street and my nineteen-year-old husband cried. He had never experienced this before. He wanted a safe place for our baby and us, and he was turned away because we were Indian.

We experienced this in 1968, five years after the civil rights movement. This kind of thing was not supposed to happen any more. I was very angry when this happened, and it is part of the reason I became radical during the sixties. In March 1969 I walked into AIM [American Indian Movement] headquarters and said, "I want to be a member." This was the beginning of a very angry, defiant time of my life. My feeling was that the government might hurt me, but I wouldn't let it hurt my children or my man. I am still enraged. I worked with AIM until 1972, for about three years. My baby was getting older, and it became harder and harder to take him along on protests, so I became less active. But I still believed strongly in causes that fight injustice.

In 1976 I heard about a program called WIN. It was set up to help poor women go to college. I picked the Head Start program as my area of study because I heard they were going to start a program at Rice, Minnesota, which is on the White Earth Reservation. It was a home-based program that worked one-on-one with my people. This was when I learned beading and basketry. I also learned about the problems of alcoholism and suicide on the reservation. I am not a drinker myself because I feel that alcohol stole my family from me when my husband was killed. I have worked with a lot of young Indian women who were alcoholic, and it's really, really hard to watch what this disease does to them and their families. I can work with these women because I am nonjudgmental about the disease. It is poison for my people, but I also understand the pain they feel that causes them to drink.

One thing I feel sad about is that the women are now the strength among my people. We are a matriarchal society, and we've lost our men in a lot of respects, either to alcoholism, to war, to poverty, or to despair. So our men do not listen to us and speak for us anymore as they used to. I prefer it the old way. But so many of them are gone that this can't happen anymore.

In our culture we were taught to listen—to our elders and to anyone who had earned the right through the wisdom of experience. But now I'm not sure if the council is listening to the women, to their voices and their hearts. I have an elder whom I listen to. I may debate with her, but I always listen to what she says. Our leaders are people who are trying very hard, but they are always criticized. I will criticize none. I love all these people who are in leadership positions in the Indian community because they are my people, but that doesn't mean I always agree with them. We are all victims, all of us. Some were victimized in one way, some in another. Some had the stamina to resist, and some did not. But we've all become victims in a very, very short time.

I don't think the blood-quantum question is valid at all. I am my grandmother's grandmother's child, as far back as it goes. No matter how white my children get, how can anyone deny that woman who is buried seven miles straight east of here? They cannot deny her. She was three-quarters Indian and one-quarter black. You can say she has no connection to me if you like, but I can't deny her. She is my history. Whatever happened to her, happened to me. Whatever happens to me, happens to my children.

I see the Indian way as a kinder, gentler way. My mother taught me that if you had five bucks, you gave it away; if there was a kid with his nose pressed against the screen door, you fed him; if a hitchhiker needed a ride, you picked him up. I didn't have a name for this way of life; it was just the right way to do things. Because of this sense of rightness, church attendance as a child was hard for me. It felt wrong. I didn't feel the sharing and giving that my mother said we should practice. The church's sharing and giving were different from what I had learned.

The sweat-lodge ceremony has been very important to me. It's like a tranquilizer that gives me peace. It's a time of giving thanks for what I have, being grateful for my ninety-nine-year-old grandmother, my children, and my friends.

I don't have to worry about being "good enough" for a while. I just am who I am. I have also been to sun-dance ceremonies with my second husband, but only as an observer. Next time I will participate. I believe I need these ceremonies to deal with the rage I often feel about the injustice I meet every day in my life and in my job.

I guess I was naive two years ago when I thought I could go down to the capital and work to make some changes. I was there from May to September, when I finally broke down and felt defeated. I came home from work and said to my husband, "I want to go home. I can't do anything here. I take four steps ahead and ten back." I felt hopeless. The Indian-white wars are alive and well. There are so many lies out there. People don't know the real story.

    I stay with my job even though I get discouraged and frustrated, because I think it is important that Indian people have an Indian person to greet them when they walk into a government office to work something out. We are in a time when many people think the answer lies in stronger laws, stricter punishment, and more prisons. But I believe many Indians are just now beginning to find peace within themselves. When this happens in the hearts of all of us, we'll have a more peaceful world. Whether we will ever see it, I don't know.

Dena Rae is a sixteen-year-old high school student in Bagley, Minnesota. She was born in Minneapolis and lived there for a few years until she moved to the Bagley area with her mother, her siblings, and her maternal grandfather. In her sophomore year, Dena was class secretary. She was also a cheerleader for varsity basketball and football. Dena was a member of SADD (Students Against Destructive Decisions) and was part of a movement to set up an Amerind Club for Native Americans. She enjoys drawing and art and was involved in an art club for a while. Presently she has taken up beading and sewing in order to finish her shawl dress to participate in powwows. Dena is interested in getting a good education, as well as the usual teenage diversions such as shopping and being with friends. She is exploring career ideas but has made no firm decisions about her future.

Dena Rae Iron Cloud
Born: July 1, 1982

I lived in Minneapolis until I was nine, when my father died. My grandfather has always lived with us, so he moved to the Bagley, Minnesota, area with my mother, my brother, Troy, and my two sisters, Laurel and Shalene. We moved into a big house right next to an egg factory. We rented it for almost five years, but when my grandfather died in July, the six-bedroom house seemed too big for us. During the winters, it was getting hard to heat; it was very expensive, even with a wood stove and electricity. My grandfather helped at first, but then he had a stroke and a heart attack. He couldn't do much after that.

My grandfather was still the man around the house, even though he couldn't do much physically and had trouble talking and understanding people. He usually stayed in his room, and we would go in to visit him. We would just talk to him or bring him food and things. Grandpa was real happy. He always had a smile on his face. My mother was the main caregiver. My grandfather had family in Texas, but I remember seeing them only once, when they all came to White Earth for a reunion. Grandpa was enrolled at White Earth.

My mother's family was not very close to us. I had "aunts" in the Cities whom I called auntie, but they may not have been real aunts. I see these aunts and uncles when I go down to the Cities. There are a lot of them, and we usually visit on holidays. Since my dad died, my mother doesn't really celebrate Christmas or anything, so she takes us down there to visit. She more or less drops us off and then goes back to Bagley, because she likes it much better away from the city. Sometimes we stay a couple weeks, or in the summer we might stay a lot longer. I have a lot of friends in Minneapolis.

Grades are important to me, but sometimes in school I feel off track. I get lazy and decide I don't need to go that day. But I try to work hard. I'd like to be in a lot more stuff, but I can't because we live so far out of town. It's hard to get to meetings.

I am usually on the honor roll, but I'm not now because I am just too lazy. I'm disappointed in myself because I would like to be in drama club and in dance line, but that takes up a lot of time. Practices at five in the morning are very early.

In school I've never really had any enemies. I get along with everybody; I've had friends in all different kinds of groups. My cousins are friends with what they call "preps" and stuff. Mostly I'm with my cousin Angel and her friends. I hang out with a lot of different friends, but most of the time we Indians just kind of stick together. One of my friends is white, and she started hanging out with Indian kids because I do. At first she was afraid of them, but now she feels she belongs. When I first got into the cheerleading squad, I caught hell from the Indians. They would tease me so bad. They would call me "white girl" and stuff. I just kind of laughed it off. I was the first Indian I know of who was a cheerleader, but now there are many more.

I don't get along that well with my sisters or my cousin Marissa. For example, my sister Shalene and I only get along when we want something from each other. Then we go back to fighting. She wants to do everything *now.* Marissa is the little mother around my house. Like the other night I went out and my mother told me to be home by midnight, and Marissa says, "No, you be home at 10:30."

My mother is very protective. She wants to know where I will be every single minute and wants me to call all the time. She gets in my face and wants to know where I'm at and whom I'm with. When my sister and I started getting into trouble, she really got protective. But I know she's only trying to watch over us and make sure we're not getting into any trouble. I also know that my mother's worries are real. I have been going with my boyfriend for about three months. We go with my friends to dances, or movies, or out to eat. But my mother worries.

Drinking is a big concern among our crowd. The "good" people, the "popular" people, everyone drinks. If there is a good party going on, I'll drink and stuff; but if I have school the next morning, I won't.

Some of my friends call me militant because of some of the things my mother taught me about my heritage. When I tell my friends what she said, they say I'm militant. Sometimes I'll be talking to my mom about something ordinary and she'll say, "Indians didn't do that back in the old days." Then I'll say, "Mom, Indians didn't play bingo back then either."

I believe that we are a very spiritual family. We don't go to church or anything, but we do follow ceremonies—of fasting, sweats, and drum dances. Mom wants to take us to a sun-dance ceremony, but I'm a little afraid of that. I'm not at all ashamed of my mother's involvement in the native ceremonies. In fact, I'm very proud. I wouldn't give up being Indian for anything. My whole family is a very proud people. We really just started getting into the traditional ceremonies when we moved up here. We began finding out things about our heritage. As my mom started learning more, she would tell it to us, and we would learn.

When my grandpa died, his funeral combined traditional ways with a Christian burial. I really don't think we should try to mix the two. There is a church in Minneapolis that tries to work together, Christian and traditional; it doesn't seem right to me.

I have to admit that clothes are important to me, too. I have a lot of clothes. If I didn't have them, I wouldn't be unhappy, and I know my friends wouldn't stop liking me or anything. But I like to shop, and I like to buy clothes that are right for me. My sisters and I have a lot of disagreements about clothes. My mother has to step in sometimes to talk to us when we're fighting about clothes.

Right now I'm working on my dancing outfit. I will have to start beading and sewing to finish it. I haven't danced much this past year because, in our tradition, we don't dance for about a year after someone close to you has died. I'm going to finish my shawl dress first and then start on my jingle dress.

We usually attend the powwows around here, like at Red Lake and Cass Lake. When we have the money, we go up to Canada to White Fish Bay or Long Prairie. It's nice to see so many Indians coming together to do something like a powwow. I really enjoy it.

One person I admire a lot is the singer Selina. I have her CD, and I've read a lot about her since she died. She was a really down-to-earth person. She didn't change because she was famous. She was the same person, on and off the stage. These are qualities I admire.

Kathleen Renee Annette

Born: April 18, 1955

Kathleen Annette is a physician who directs the Bemidji-area office of the Indian Health Service. An enrolled member at White Earth, she received her doctor of medicine degree from the University of Minnesota, completed her residency at the Duluth Family Practice Center, and spent four years in family practice on the Leech Lake Reservation. She lives in Bemidji.

According to my mother, who speaks the language fluently, my Indian name is pronounced ANHI-koo-biday, which means "to bind or tie together." I was the firstborn, so I was given this name to bind together the union of my mother and father. I was born in the hospital on the White Earth Reservation but lived there for just a short period of time. I grew up on the Red Lake Reservation.

Red Lake is the only closed reservation in the state. I think that in many ways the traditions are very much alive there. With the exception of learning the language fluently, I think we were raised almost as traditionally as you could be in this day and age in terms of values, culture, the dance, and the song. Red Lake fostered a strong Indian identity for everyone in my family. That's how we identify ourselves: I'm an Indian, I'm a woman, and I'm a physician, but I am an Indian first. I never doubted who I was.

It was a very good life. Respect was very much a part of how we were raised. We had a strong nuclear family. Alcohol was not part of my family. Neither of my parents drank, and that, I think, was a critical factor in our upbringing.

We also had a very strong extended family—aunts, uncles, and cousins all over the place. For many years, we had elders living in the home as part of our extended family. My Great-Uncle Al came back to the reservation, moved in with us, and lived in our home until he died. My Grandma Big Bear and my uncle, who lived in White Earth, would come and stay at any time. That's how we were raised, and those values continue to sustain me to this day.

I'm an Indian person living in this society, and I'm very comfortable being an Indian, on or off the reservation. I went away for twelve years for my schooling, but my goal was always to get back home, work for Indian people and Indian health, and be with my family.

I'm fortunate because I come from a very bright family, and we've all got different motivations to do different things. When we were brought up, there were two or three things we never thought twice about. One of them was that we were going to college. Many kids' parents would say, "You have to graduate from high school because that's the law." That's not how we were raised: "Well, when you finish college, then you can start thinking about what you're really going to do in your life." That was from both folks, very strong. So we all finished college. We didn't realize that college was optional.

I was in about the fifth grade when I started wanting to be a doctor. My Grandma Big Bear was a medicine woman, so I always knew that we had medicine in our family. After finishing my residency, I practiced on the Leech Lake Reservation for about four years as a primary-care family practitioner. I loved it! Then I was offered the position of chief medical officer of the Bemidji-area office of the Indian Health Service, and because I was ready to take on some new challenges, I accepted it.

The Bemidji-area office is a central administrative office that covers three states [Michigan, Minnesota, Wisconsin] and serves thirty-two tribes. I continued to practice while filling the chief-medical-officer position, but then the directorship of the Bemidji-area office opened. I've held that position for the past three years. It's primarily an administrative position. It's fascinating. I tried keeping up both my practice and my administrative duties for awhile, but I was called out of clinic so much that it wasn't fair to my patients, so I haven't been actively practicing medicine for the past three years.

I think it will take about two more years here to complete most of my initiatives and objectives. Then they'll need new blood for new ideas. That's when I'll start phasing out.

What to do then is a big question for me. Right now, I've met a lot of the goals I had set for myself to achieve by retirement. But since I'm only thirty-nine years old and I've already accomplished many of them, I'm in the position of establishing a whole new realm of goals and dreams.

I think one of my dreams is to someday practice on the White Earth Reservation at the new clinic they'll be getting in two years. I have some very strong commitments to the state, to my reservation, and to my community. When I was practicing at Leech Lake, I also did a lot of teaching with medical students and gave them a reservation experience. I would like to start doing that again.

I like to teach. I've become a mentor to several Indian medical students, and it's just kind of evolved. It's not unusual for me to get a caller who says,

"Kathy, I went into an autopsy today and I freaked out. You're the only one I can talk to about it." And then we work through those feelings.

I spend hours on the phone talking to students on a one-to-one basis. I don't even think about that as mentoring. It's just being a responsible Indian person. People did that for me, so I will do that for them.

It has taken me a while to figure out that Indian people respect the Creator through the created. If my sister makes a pot for me and gives it to me as a gift, I love, respect, and cherish that pot because it's something she created and gave to me. The Indian values are not instilled in any kind of formal or structured way. You just live it; you live the life. A powwow is a great church. Community gatherings are great churches.

There isn't a book you can read to learn about it. There are everyday things I do or go to that I don't think of in terms of traditional or contemporary Indian values. For example, take an honoring ceremony. My girlfriend recently wanted to arrange one for a man who just moved into the community to be the first Indian defense attorney in our region. He'll be given gifts—wild rice or venison or blankets or an eagle feather. If a pipe carrier comes, they might choose to smoke a pipe to honor him. It's not planned out. It's not a formal itinerary. People will come with their own ideas of how to honor this person, and it could be in any number of ways.

These things just happen within the texture of my life. I don't separate them out as cultural events. It's all just a part of the life I lead.

When I was practicing medicine, the medicine man and I, as far as I was concerned, were kind of partners. Sometimes we would talk, but otherwise we would operate independently. We would cross-refer. There were some things a medicine man could not help people with so he would refer them to me.

Sometimes someone will say to me, "I've got this illness or disease I want treated medically, but my family is not happy with me because we are traditional." I'll tell them, "Well, I'll give this medicine man a call. He will work with your family." You realize you don't just treat a patient; you treat a whole family or, in some situations, a whole tribe.

Sometimes Western culture doesn't understand much about Indian culture. When I was doing my residency and a person would come in with a heart attack, I knew there would be twenty people sitting in the waiting room because that's the way it should be. All those Indians sitting out there caused great chaos with the coronary-care unit. I'd have to explain it to the staff. When my dad had a heart attack, twenty of us were there around the clock because that's the way it should be.

Diabetes, heart disease, unintentional injuries, and alcoholism are our biggest health problems. The biggest killer for us is alcohol. It creates a dysfunction and a disharmony that we just cannot adequately combat today. Alcohol has caused more imbalance in our lives than anything else. It's the biggest challenge we have right now. Take alcohol out of the picture, let our culture and value systems flourish, and we could do anything we wanted to as a people. But how do we get rid of it? We are trying to deal with it in a number of different ways. All are successful to a degree, but there's no one perfect answer.

We are great enablers. We are taught to take care of each other. There is some alcoholism in our extended family. On one hand, from all the training I've had, I know that we should not be enablers. I've had all the book learning. Yet being the person I am, of course I am going to help take care of them. I do it, but I'm mad about it. It's frustrating.

You can become very consumed by medicine, but that's unhealthy. Medicine is what I do, not who I am; I work very hard at staying aware of this. The downside of medicine for me is the amount of time I gave in training for it, including the 80-to-120-hour workweek of a resident. I have no children. It was a choice back then not to take that route because I was just so busy with everything else. And now, looking forty in the face, I see that as a downside, too. Another downside sometimes is losing friends who are my patients. When I lose someone, I have to go through the case very thoroughly to make sure there wasn't anything more I could have done. I never whip myself afterward, but I want to have done my very best.

My father died in 1977 at a young age from a heart attack. It was a very sad time for me because he had his heart attack at my college graduation. He recovered and lived six more weeks, but then he had a second heart attack. If I look back at any particular point in my life, that was the most traumatic, the most emotionally difficult time for me ever. Now he's remembered in our family with stories. The grandchildren and the little ones know about Grandpa. He's just part of the circle now.

Lorna Jean LaGue is the human resources manager-tribal liaison for the Shooting Star Casino in Mahnomen, Minnesota. She has worked in the personnel field since graduating from high school and has also attended Moorhead State University. Lorna is a divorced mother of two children. She sees the casino industry as providing the reservation with vital resources to alleviate the cycle of poverty. Making a difference in the lives of Native American people is very important to her.

Lorna Jean LaGue
Born: August 21, 1964

I look back on my life and say that I did everything backwards. I had my first child when I was seventeen, got married at eighteen, started a job, and then went to college. I may have done everything backwards, but I learned a lot that way.

I am the human resources manager-tribal liaison for the Shooting Star Casino in Mahnomen. I started out as the personnel manager and was involved in the hiring from day one. At any given time, we have up to a thousand employees. I have a department of thirteen people. I have someone to take care of hiring, firing, and benefits and to act as an employee counselor. My position is twofold because I'm also the tribal liaison. The tribal government relies on me to be their hands-on person here. If they have questions about a Native American employee, I'll answer them. I also work with overseeing the financial statements, figuring out why the profits are up or down.

This is a very stressful position. When you mix a casino industry and tribal government together, you have a heck of a mess on your hands! I rely on the serenity prayer. With the growth we experienced the first couple of years, we were lucky if we got crisis management done. This place is open twenty-four hours a day. I'm not here twenty-four hours a day, so when I come in the morning, I've missed two shifts of work. We immediately play catch-up. Monday mornings are terrible because I've missed so many shifts from the weekend.

It cost millions of dollars to build and equip this place. People think we're rolling in money, but we're not. They don't realize what it costs to run a place like this. Our payroll is in excess of thirteen million dollars a year. The initial building and setup costs were in excess of twenty million dollars. The operational costs are enormous. Some of the ways the tribal government uses its profits include building new housing and a youth sports/recreation facility in Nay-tah-waush and also subsidizing some of the funding sources that have fallen short at White Earth.

The White Earth Reservation had more than 90 percent unemployment. Most of the jobs on the reservation were professional jobs that required degrees. We didn't have Native American employees coming into these positions because they didn't have the qualifications, the degree, or the work experience. When we started the casino, it was a different philosophy. This place was built on the idea of providing training and an opportunity to teach. I like that challenge because I realize there's the potential to make a difference. We came here and started training and teaching people. When we hire people, we not only have to teach them how to do their jobs but also how to be employees. They haven't had jobs before, and they need to learn this. We had to teach things that most people take for granted. It feels wonderful to be a part of the change.

Prior to this position, I was the personnel manager for the White Earth Reservation, and I was responsible for sending out job announcements, hiring people, and interviewing. I was only twenty-two or twenty-three years old. Raising a child when you're young makes you grow up fast. I worked there for a few years and then moved to my current position. While working at White Earth, I was also attending Moorhead State. When the reservation decided to open up a casino, I had to put college on hold because I just didn't have the time. I've never gone back for my degree. I've already proven myself to the necessary people, and I don't need a degree behind my name. I don't think it's something I have to do to get ahead in the world.

I was born in Mahnomen and have lived around here all my life. I am the oldest of three children. My mother is full-blooded Chippewa Indian, and my father is almost full-blooded German. Because of these two diverse cultures, I come from a mixed background. Coming from that background taught me a lot; I've learned to accept all different types of people. What's inside of them matters more to me than the color of their skin. My parents had a lot to do with this.

My parents are hard workers. They work seven days a week in their own business and are very independent people. Because of their different cultural backgrounds, they pretty much stuck to themselves. In their generation, interracial marriage was just starting to become acceptable, but they had some problems with their families. Because of this, they weren't family oriented. I know all my aunts, uncles, and cousins, but we never spent a lot of time with them. Now I look at my nieces and nephews and realize we all spend so much time together. Perhaps my parents just didn't have the time. They were working sunrise until sunset.

My father came from the old philosophy that your son is the person who carries your name and is your right-hand person. My being the oldest but not a boy had a big influence on my life. My parents were more strict with me because I was the oldest and, therefore, was setting the precedent. My younger brother was the special one of the family and was favored. I sensed this when I was growing up, and I think it taught me independence. I have a survivor-type personality.

When I was in school, there was still a lot of prejudice. Even though I'm obviously Native American, I was able to fit into both cultures. Actually, if I experienced any prejudice, it was probably the opposite way—because I was not Indian enough to some people. I became more aware of my culture in my high school years. I started being active in the Indian Club and things like that. I remember my dad asking me, "How come you're not in the German Club?" I didn't really have an answer for him, just that the Indian Club interested me more at the time.

As a teenager, I became real rebellious. Looking back now, I think I did that purposely because of the relationship with my brother. I learned to have a mind of my own and did what I wanted to, whether my parents liked it or not. I wouldn't listen to anyone and wanted to learn everything for myself. I wish I could do it all over today! When I was sixteen, I became pregnant with my daughter, and she was born when I was seventeen. By that time, I had moved out of the house and was living with friends. I was going to do this myself! I dropped out of school and was very independent.

During this time, I had a really good mentor named Verna Millage. I credit a lot of my own success back to her. She cared enough to get me back in school. Verna was an Indian-student counselor, and it was her job to try to alleviate the dropout rate. When she came out to see me, I respected her enough to know I had to listen. She would pick me up for school and bring me home again at the end of the day. I've always had good grades and was on the honor roll. She knew I had potential and that if I didn't get off my butt and get moving, it was going to be wasted. At an awards ceremony for the graduating Indian students, I presented her with a dozen roses. I remember her being very touched. By that time, I realized what she had done for me.

My husband and I divorced in 1987 or 1988. We had different goals in life and were opposites in many ways. At that time, I found I had a lot of extra time on my hands. Knowing that Verna Millage was the recruiter for Moorhead State University, I decided to enroll. For a couple of years, I raised two kids, worked full-time at White Earth, and went to school full-time. I did that until 1991, my senior year. As I said, I had to drop out of college when the reservation opened the Shooting Star Casino. We were so busy that we were lucky if we got to go home to sleep at night.

During the last four years, I've done nothing but work. This past summer, I evaluated my situation. Four years of this is enough. I've had one vacation, and I don't have the time to spend with my children and family that I want. I'm trying to switch gears right now. I don't think I want to commit the rest of my life to my job the way I've done the past four years. The price is too high. My kids are growing up. I'll probably stay working here forever, but I wouldn't mind being an assistant manager. I guess you might say I'm in kind of a transition.

I've recently begun quilting. It's a challenge and an accomplishment. It also allows me time to think. My children and family are important to me. Professionally, making a difference in our culture is important. I think that with the casino here, there is a potential to change the poverty cycle of the reservation. We need this change to get back on our feet and get moving forward. I believe it's important to spend time on things that make a difference.

Theresa Olsen

Born: March 2, 1951

Theresa Olsen has been an educator for many years. Even before she graduated in 1980 from Bemidji State University, she held jobs in schools and worked with children. She was born on the White Earth Reservation and has three brothers and four sisters. Her two sons and two daughters are young adults who are employed in the area; her youngest son still lives at home. Theresa has always known she would become a teacher and has found it a very satisfying career.

There is an enormous old building near White Earth that used to be the mission school, run by nuns. That is where my mother went to school and actually lived until her senior year. She didn't go home for summers as some kids did. She just stayed there all the time. My mother now lives near the Cass Lake Reservation. She is a schoolteacher in Cass Lake.

My mother raised eight children and then went to college after we were grown. In fact, she graduated from college just a few years before I did. We both went to Bemidji State University. Mother told me once that she had worked as an aide in the school for a while, and she knew she could do what the teachers did. That motivated her to go to college and become a teacher. She graduated in 1975, and I graduated in 1980.

My father did a lot of different things, from carpentry to trapping. We all lived in a small house on North Twin Lake. The house had three rooms and no electricity. We had an indoor pump to draw our water. We lived there until I was seventeen, when the first housing project was completed. One of my sisters lives in that same spot now.

Almost all of us are still in the area, and we are involved in a variety of things. Two of us are teachers. Two of my brothers work at the casino, one as a pit boss and the other doing personnel work. My oldest sister is a cook for the Head Start program in Minneapolis. Another sister is a home health aide for the public health service; she helps the elderly and also works with young families. And another one works as an emergency medical technologist for the ambulance service in Nay-tah-waush. Except for Kathy, who lives in Minneapolis, we are all close enough to get together on Sunday mornings at my mother's house for coffee and visiting.

Although I didn't start college right after high school in Mahnomen, I had a lot of experience with kids. I was raising my own, and I worked as a teacher's aide and helped with 4-H projects and summer programs. I taught arts and crafts; my specialty is beadwork. When I did start school in Bemidji, I shared rides with others who were making the fifty-mile commute. My children were in school, so I arranged my schedule to run from eight in the morning to four in the afternoon. There was always family around to help out with the children.

Becoming a teacher was something I had always wanted to do. When I was young, I read a lot, and I guess there's never been any doubt in my mind that I would go to college. I took time out to have my children, but I always knew I would continue my education.

I didn't have any trouble getting a job because I did my student teaching in Bagley. While I was there, they needed to hire three more teachers because they had so many students. I finished my student teaching on a Friday, and the following Monday I started teaching a class. I was happy to get this job. I really enjoyed teaching. My friend Gail and I used to talk about how lucky we were to be paid for something we liked doing so much. Physically, I remember it was challenging, but I enjoyed the work, and everyone helped that first year. I have been teaching now for fourteen years, and I still love it.

I've seen kids change over the years. There are a lot more kids coming through now who are having troubles, and I see the parents struggling with this. They want their kids to do well, and they try to set good examples. I see many more learning problems than I used to. A few years ago, I would have one child a year who needed a lot of modifications; now it seems like a third of my class is like that. The class size has usually been about twenty, but this year I have twenty-six, and one of them is in a wheelchair and is legally blind. When there were fewer students, there was more space, and we could do more hands-on kinds of things. Discipline is harder with a bigger class. The respect is not there as it used to be. You can hear second-grade kids swearing at teachers. You never heard that ten years ago.

I think being an Indian person has made it easier for me to relate with some of the families. I know the kids and their families. I am the only Indian staff in the elementary school right now. The Indian students often come back to talk with me. Many of them have a lot of troubles and need someone to talk to.

Sometimes it's hard being the only Indian staff. It's not that the others are prejudiced, but I need to be around Indian people sometimes. A very good friend of mine, who was Lebanese, was killed not long ago. We used to do a lot of teaching together. She and I attended a ten-day art-and-archeology seminar in the Southwest one summer. We visited the Navaho, the Hopi, and the Sunni reservations. When we got back, we tried a lot of new ideas with our classes. This was exciting and fun, and I miss her.

I've been divorced about fifteen years. My mother told me once that if I really wanted something, I had to take care of it. She said not to depend on anyone else. I remember that I always wanted a house of my own. And if I wanted this, I would have to do it myself. I haven't spent much time waiting for other people to do things for me. If I wanted something, I went after it.

Because of my mother's background in the mission school, all of us children were baptized Catholic. After I married, I became an Episcopalian. Religion has always been an important part of my life. I worked with a lot of the youth when my kids were younger. I've been a member of the bishop's committee and the Episcopal church women's committee and have held offices in both of them. I suppose there are people around who still practice the traditional beliefs, but I personally don't know any of them.

I am not saying that there is not a renewed interest in traditional Indian beliefs. I believe there is. It just has not been a big part of my own life. I have attended many powwows in the area, and I used to dance when I was younger. I am proud of my heritage, and I value the wisdom of my culture, even though I am not active.

My work has brought me some experiences that I feel good about. For example, another teacher and I applied for a grant for a summer program for Indian youths for science and math enhancement. We ran this program for four summers. We would work with fifth and sixth graders right after school was out in the spring. There were also a lot of parents involved. We would choose a science project to work on, and then we would take them down to Itasca State Park and camp for a week while they did their projects, gathered data, and learned how to live with each other. When we returned to Bagley, the kids would work on computers and put their projects on paper. While they were writing the reports, we would go on mini-trips, like to the mortuary, the museum, and state parks, so they could see firsthand how math and science were used in the world. At the end of the fourth week, we took the kids (usually about twenty of them) to Minneapolis, where we visited the Minnesota Science Museum, and the students gave oral reports to a group of scientists. We finished up with a little banquet and a Twins game.

    Being employed in the schools gave me many opportunities to travel. I used to take kids on trips with an Episcopal priest. We did a ten-day backpacking trip in the Boundary Waters area; we hiked the Grand Canyon with some seniors; we went backpacking into the Canadian Rockies in Banff National Park; and we went sailing from Maine to Rhode Island, watching whales. Lately, my son Andy and I have traveled some. His favorite place is the Southwest, on top of the mesas. We love natural places without crowds of people. There is so much to see and do in this country.

Blanche Turner is an elder who still lives in the area where she was born. She was enrolled at birth as a White Earth tribal member. She has four children, who visit her frequently, but she has lived alone since the death of her husband a year ago. Blanche has become widely known for her needlework skill and has created quilts that are prized by people all over the country; she still does this work on a limited basis. Blanche's memories span a lifetime of change for her people. She values her family and her heritage, and she regrets some of the changes she sees in modern society.

Blanche Turner
Born: July 29, 1918

My grandfather was a farmer. He was Scottish and Irish and was born in Virginia. He headed north when he was just fifteen years old. He said he was going up there to marry a tall schoolmarm. He did this, and she *was* tall, taller than my grandfather. She was Chippewa and was allotted land near Lengby, Minnesota.

My dad worked the farm with his dad, and I lived there until I was about five. They had to clear the land by hand. It was a big farm, and my grandfather raised pigs and shipped out the meat. In the winter, he would go to Canada and trap. He would stay there all winter and come home in the spring and farm. There were twelve of us, a big family. These were hard years, during the Depression. My parents lost three of their children when they were very young, two girls and a boy. The farm was in the family for a long time, but when my father died, none of the boys wanted to farm. I wish we could have kept it. My boys would have farmed it.

We moved to Nay-tah-waush when I was five, and I went to school there until the seventh grade. Then I went to Pipestone, Minnesota, because they didn't have buses back then to take us to high school in Mahnomen. If you wanted to go to high school there, you had to live in Mahnomen and pay your room and board. My brothers were going to Pipestone, and a lot of other kids I knew were also going to the government school. Most kids stayed right at the school from September through May, and then they went back home for the summer. Some of them, who didn't have parents or who came from broken homes, stayed right there and made the school their home. My parents really didn't want me to leave to go to school, but I put up a big fuss and they let me go. I stayed there through the ninth grade.

I remember the beautiful setting in Pipestone where the school put on pageants during the summer. It was like an amphitheater. It was really something.

All the experiences at the boarding schools were pleasant, even though we had some very strict matrons. I remember one very clearly because I thought she had an evil mind. Some of the boys who went to school with braids were made to cut them off. And my cousin told me that at bath time, five or six of the girls had to bathe in the same water. My cousin said she was always the last one.

I learned a lot at school. I think the courses were about the same as public school. But I also lost my hand while I was there. I was working in the laundry, trying to feed flannel shirts into the mangle when my fingers got caught. They couldn't get them out, so I lost them. I was in ninth grade, about thirteen or fourteen years old. For a while, I wished that I had never gone to school, but then I thought, "Well, I have to live with it." And I really wanted to finish school.

Flandreau, South Dakota, was the site of a school I attended for my sophomore and junior years. Then, during the last year, I went home for Christmas and didn't go back. I worked for two years before I finished school in Haskell, Kansas. When I returned home, I started school in Bemidji, but my government loan didn't go through, so I had to quit.

I'm not sure why I was so set on finishing school; there were lots of things to discourage me. For one thing, my parents didn't want me to go because I had two little sisters who had died. They didn't want to lose me, too. One of my sisters died from choking and the other one from convulsions. It is too bad people didn't know CPR back then. The closest doctor was in Mahnomen, and it was hard to get to him. My dad had a car, a Model T, and when my older brother got sick with polio, my dad had to take him to Fosston, Minnesota, to find out what he had. My brother is over eighty years old now and has a very crippled leg with a bad limp. But he doesn't let it bother him; he still traps and is very active. His leg is like my hand; I learned from watching him not to let it bother me. I even sewed for my kids. I did everything. Of course, my husband was really good. He helped me when he was home, especially after he retired.

I got married in 1940, when I returned from Bemidji. My husband and I were married for fifty-four years and had four children—two boys, Orville and Doyle, and two girls, Shelley and Colleen. My husband worked road construction, which took him away from home a lot—Wisconsin, Montana, Iowa. In the summer, the kids and I would go with him. That was our vacation, and it was fun. Every spring we just loaded up the car and took off. One summer we lived in Bozeman, Montana. It was so pretty there that we didn't want to come home.

I have seen a lot of changes over the years. I often think that Nay-tah-waush isn't a safe place to live anymore. It used to be that everyone knew each other. We could just lock the door and go away for a while and it would be fine. When my son wanted me to go to Florida where he lives, I told him I can't leave my house. Two years ago, before my husband died, we were getting ready to go to church, and when we went into the garage, the car was gone. It was stolen right out of the garage.

When my husband and I were raising the children, we were very busy. I even cooked at the school for a while. Then I got hired for twenty hours a week at Green Thumb, a place for senior citizens. They were making quilts there, and I would help them. They used to tell me to make a star quilt, but I said, "Never." I thought it was too much of a challenge. But one day I decided to give it a try. I have been quilting ever since. Now my quilts are all over the country and even in England.

I sew quilts for family and friends, and a lot of them are special orders. I do pillows, too. When my husband died a year ago, I didn't know what to do with all his neckties, so I made pillows for my sons. They like them. My husband and I bought clothes and everything from the money I made from my quilts.

I am still quilting, and I stay busy with that and church, and I go to the senior citizens' center for meals. I am very close with my children, but after my husband died, it has been lonesome. You feel alone after a funeral. So many people come, then all of a sudden there's nobody. I am grateful for my quilting.

Leah is the youngest of five girls who grew up in a very poor family. Her mother died of alcoholism when Leah was thirteen years old; she was raised largely by her older sisters, and she spent a year with foster parents. She knew for a long time that she would be an attorney. Leah credits her basic family values, some significant teachers and counselors, and the Upward Bound program for helping her continue to believe in herself. She feels a great deal of empathy for the people with whom she works, and she understands the cultural barriers they encounter in the legal system. She has attended several schools and majored in political science and Indian studies with a minor in business, and she has a law degree from the University of Wisconsin. Leah lives with her partner near Cass Lake and has two children, a son and a daughter.

Leah Carpenter
Born: March 26, 1958

Losing my mother at age thirteen was really, really difficult. I was "too cool" at that age to deal with the loss, and it resulted in a lot of bad behavior: drinking, skipping school, and many other things. While I was living in a foster home in Blackduck, the director of the Upward Bound program became one of my mentors. He asked if I'd be interested in attending a private boarding school in Massachusetts called the Northfield Mount Herman School. I was selected because of my academic record and the fact that they were looking for poor Indian kids from the Midwest to attend their school. It was a good plan, but after just one year I began to feel that I had to get back home. I also tried Carleton College in Northfield, Minnesota, on a scholarship, but that lasted only two days. I really needed my family, so I returned and worked for the state Indian scholarship program for a year and then attended Bemidji State University. I went there for a couple of years but didn't focus much on studying. Social life was more important. I ended up getting a job with the Minnesota Chippewa Tribe working in an office that dealt with the settlement of land claims on the reservation, which eventually resulted in the White Earth Land Settlement Act. I did that for about three years and in the meantime had my son, Kenny. After working for three years and becoming a mother, I went back to school a much more serious student and graduated in 1985. Even though I knew what my career direction was, I took a year off between college and law school, mostly because of Kenny. I was a single parent; Kenny's father had died when Kenny was three, and I wanted to wait until my son was in school full-time before I entered. I did some work that year for Leech Lake on their land claims while I was raising Kenny and getting ready for law school.

After graduating from law school in 1989, I worked for a year in Minneapolis as an administrative and law clerk for Judge Stephen D. Swanson and then came home to work for the Anishinabe Legal Services for the next six years. I worked in the trenches on behalf of Indian people in the legal system in this area. I had always wanted to work for Indian people with my law degree, and that's what I got to do at Legal Services, but working in the legal system in the community where I grew up was hard at times. It was difficult to go in as a lawyer to face judges whom I was in front of as a juvenile. Running into court personnel who remarked about my family or my past in disparaging comments was hard. I don't know if it was because I was an Indian person or just because I was dirt poor, but the classism-type stuff seemed to come up and I heard things that were hard to take on a personal level. It really sent me into some kind of internalized searching. Also, observing how Indian people are treated in our legal system in this area is disheartening. Because of the many institutional barriers, justice is often hard to come by.

I just started working for the White Earth Tribal Council about three or four weeks ago and will be heading up the Constitutional Reform Project. My past work on land claim projects has turned out to be a gold mine of information for me on this present job. I did a lot of digging, a lot of research, and a lot of reading. I tried to compile all the treaties that have impacted White Earth. Some of the documents I found were significant legislative acts and court cases that have affected White Earth and the people there. While working in land claims, one thing I really took to heart and firmly believe in is if you don't know your own history, you're condemned to repeat it. To me, the land claim work was very significant because it allowed me the opportunity to research the creation of the reservation and find out about my ancestors and my history as a member of White Earth. Many questions remain. For example, where is my grandmother's allotment, and my grandfather's? What happened to them? Were they part of the illegal transfers? I certainly think we need to start with an understanding of all the history as a base for any kind of constitutional reform. We need to inform the community of our distant history and also about some of the more recent history with the former tribal council and the way they operated. There was a lot of suppression of documents and a lot of information withheld from the community. Government accountability is probably the top issue for everyone, not just on White Earth but all over Indian country in Minnesota. I want to recognize that and change that in this process we are going through with the constitutional reform. I see my role as being more of a facilitator than anything else. What we intend to do is get the tribal council and the people working together to come up with something that will work for all of us. Educating and informing twenty-four thousand members of White Earth scattered all over the place is a very big job, but these issues have to be put to the entire population and we hope they will come out and vote. I find this challenging and exciting. Education of the tribal members and the public is so important, and it's our first order of business. There's a great deal of work ahead.

Looking back on the latest three generations of my family helps to explain where I am today with my beliefs, interests, and spirituality. My grandmother, for instance, spoke Ojibwe fluently, but because she had been "Christianized," she did not encourage her children to speak the language or to learn the traditional ways. I think my mother and her siblings were taught that being an Indian was not a good thing and that it was better to act more like a white person. Much of my heritage wasn't learned until I got to college. And how many of us go to college?

Both my children have received Indian names, and I've tried to teach them a little about the natural ways and have them participate in the powwows and dancing. My daughter and I have jingle dresses, and my son, Kenny, was a dancer, too, when he was younger. All my elders have passed away, so my family has had to rely on Kenny's grandmother and that side of the family to learn about traditions. Kenny's father was an almost full-blood from Enger, a very traditional village in Leech Lake. His whole family knows a lot about our history, and I've learned from them. It has been important to Kenny, Tara, and me to keep in contact with this side of the family.

Another important person in my life is my present partner, Pete. We've been together for a long time; according to Indian custom, we're considered married. In the eyes of the community, we are. Pete is the father of my five-year-old daughter, Tara. Pete is a full-blood from a traditional village in Red Lake. He was a product of that time when Indian children were taken away and raised in foster homes. He has distinct memories of that. He was separated from his parents and his siblings. The whole family is still trying to overcome the trauma this created. They are coming back together now as adults and re-creating their family.

We have a very intertribal family. I'm enrolled at White Earth, Kenny at Leech Lake, and Tara at Red Lake, with her father.

I've tried to return and thank the people who helped me—teachers, counselors, and, of course, my sisters, who were my core support. I think that every child growing up needs to have somebody to give encouragement and love. These beliefs have helped me in raising my own children. It has been difficult at times, especially when I was a single parent. It has been more difficult in our society to raise a daughter than a son. There are so many images out there of girls being abused sexually, physically, emotionally, and not just on TV but in real life. Girls are having babies at age fourteen or fifteen and trying to raise them alone when they are still children themselves. I'm trying to get my daughter to see that she is a good person and that she deserves to be treated respectfully. She's very young yet, but I would like her to understand that the traditional roles of the Indian man are gone and that is what creates much of the dysfunction and abuse from men.

Many men who come back to their homes after having been removed as children don't have any idea what it means to be an Indian person. They've been ripped out of their culture and deprived of their language. They are struggling so hard inside to find out who they really are. Naturally, this affects how they relate to other people, including their own children.

Thelma Wang
Born: February 25, 1941

Thelma Wang is a social worker, both professionally and personally. She is very aware of the needs of her people. Her background has prepared her well for this work; the rich experiences of her life have made her sensitive to families and children. She is aware of political action but is not involved in it, choosing instead to be involved in the "front-lines" work of helping families and children directly. She believes strongly in giving children the information and guidance they need about family heritage and spirituality. Thelma has personally faced many devastating physical problems, which have made her empathetic to those with whom she works .

As a child, I moved around a lot with my family because my dad worked construction. We lived in several different towns in Montana and Wyoming, but mostly we wintered in Fargo, North Dakota. My memories are most clear of the higher elementary grades, when we lived in the Golden Ridge area in Fargo. I was the oldest of four children, two boys and two girls. When I was about thirteen, one of my brothers was accidentally killed in a gun tragedy. He was nine. It was terrible. Many of our relatives came to give us support. My brother is buried at the Episcopal Church Cemetery.

I was born on the reservation, and even though we've lived in many different places, my roots are there. I made a decision that my children were not going to be uprooted when they started school. We were in Wisconsin when my oldest entered school, so we stayed there. I bought a home in Frederic, Wisconsin, and that's where I raised my six children.

I had my first child when I was fifteen and married my baby's father when I was sixteen. I was so young. I believed at first that even though the marriage was somewhat of a disaster, I had to stick it out. My husband drank a lot and forged checks to keep drinking. I finally decided I had enough. I thought it was my job to raise the kids and be the stabilizer. But I got tired of broken promises.

Then I met a man I believed was good, and in his own way, he was. But what I got was just a different kind of abuse. The first marriage was abandonment and neglect; the second was physical and emotional abuse. In 1980 I decided I wasn't going to be beaten any more. So we just moved away. My youngest boy was about fifteen then. We just packed up everything that meant anything to me in our big, old, rusty Oldsmobile and went to live with my brother near Nay-tah-waush.

I had earned my GED [graduate equivalency degree] in Wisconsin so I could work. Now I had to make a choice. There wasn't much incentive to work back then because any money I made reduced my grant. It was better for me to stay home and take care of my kids. But I did take a job as a nurse's aide at the Mahnomen Nursing Home. My boss was encouraging me to go back to school for nurse's training when I had a heart attack.

It was good I was back home when this happened because I needed my family to help me recover. My children chose to stay in Wisconsin, but we see each other and talk on the phone when we need to. When I get lonesome, I just pack up on a Friday night and go up there and stay until Sunday.

I had the heart attack in 1985, and when I recovered I worked for a while at a group home. I noticed when I was there that most of the social workers were non-Indian. I never saw an Indian social worker. The kids all had problem families, and the social workers would set up case plans that were not culturally sensitive. Basically, the foster parents were set up to fail. It was a biased system. It wasn't understood that the children's need was to be back with their people and their parents. So I decided I wanted to be a social worker to try to save these kids from being in the system so long and ending up in group homes; these experiences left them angry and acting out behaviorally.

I had a bad car accident while I was going to school, and the physicians were concerned because of my previous heart attack. But I came through it and was soon working full-time at the group home and going to school full-time, too. Then in November 1991, I was very frightened by an incident that literally left me speechless. I couldn't talk. It was very scary. This turned out to be a stroke, which showed up on a CT scan.

The next few months were pretty shaky for me. I was afraid I would have another stroke. I was determined to finish school, though, because I was so close. I worked hard, and my teachers worked with me because I was near the end of my studies. My son and his wife moved in with us to help. I would go into the bedroom at night and just force myself to read the newspaper to stimulate my brain.

I told my daughter-in-law, "I'm so scared my brain is going to die. It's not going to rejuvenate if I don't stimulate it to work." In the nursing home, we always said that if the patients were allowed to just sit in the corner and be sad and weren't stimulated to talk, to remember, to get angry, or anything, their brains would die. That's what I was afraid of. It was hard. But I got so I could read, write, underline important parts, and then read them out loud so I would remember.

The health problems weren't over yet. I graduated in 1995, even though I was having severe problems with getting tired and catching my breath. I would drive from Waubun to school and get there forty-five minutes early so I could sleep in the parking lot before going to class. I thought maybe I had asthma, but then a doctor gave me a stress test and found out I had blockages. Then came the bypass surgery and recovery.

As I got better, I volunteered at the Indian Child Welfare Program. This is where I did my internship. I was even paid for my work through the Foster Care Program. Now I am a reunification specialist. I work with families that have an ongoing case plan. Followup is so important. Sometimes these families need to be visited or given a little extra push to complete the last steps. Sometimes they need transportation for appointments. Sometimes they need referrals to other agencies.

There are always problems when a family gets back together. Someone needs to be there to just keep an eye on things, to encourage. Parents get overwhelmed, too, especially if they have their own personal issues to handle, like chemical and alcohol abuse. All the members need support. Sometimes a placement has to be made outside the home. When this happens, we place the child in a home where at least one of the parents is an enrolled member. This way the child does not lose both parents and culture.

Sometimes I end up doing some rather unusual things, like helping to mow lawns so a renter won't get evicted. If I get too involved, my husband might say, "Now, Ma, I think you're getting a little too involved here." Then sometimes he helps me with what I have to do.

Now it seems that they [the federal government] want more master's degree social workers. I don't want to do this. I'm where I want to be right now. I don't want to be a boss. I want to be out there in the field, working with these people who trust me because I've faced many of the same problems they have. The treatment and help I received have been very meaningful. Now I can pass this on.

Because I was not raised on the reservation, I see that part of the problem we face is that the Native Americans live their lives one day at a time, but the non-Indians plan, plan, plan. In our education setup, the kids bump into this difference when they leave Nay-tah-waush and enter Mahnomen. The kids call it racism. Maybe it is, but it also is just ignorance of the two ways of life. I hope I can teach both at the same time. Where better to start than with the kids?

Sometimes I wonder why I have kept on the path that I'm on. I think I must be destined to do what I'm doing because of everything that has happened to me. I've always said, "I'm here for some reason, and God doesn't want me up there yet, because I've been through so much. Apparently, I'm not done, because I'm still working on it." I'm happy being involved with my people and the kids. Wherever I can help, I want to help—not to be a caretaker but just to help.

Mary Harper is the academic coordinator of the Native Americans into Medicine Program at Bemidji State University. She lives in Cass Lake, Minnesota, in a large house with her parents, her children, and a nephew. She is working on a postgraduate degree at Bemidji State University in educational administration.

Mary Harper
Born: June 18, 1961

My job is demanding and takes a lot of time, so my free time is mostly spent with my children, who are being home-schooled. My mother spends the mornings working with them on English, social studies, and that part of the curriculum; then when I get home, I teach them the math and sciences. We receive very good materials through the mail, and the kids take standardized tests at the end of the year. They are doing very well. We don't take any money from the state for the home-schooling, but we do use the public library quite extensively. The curriculum packets cost about three hundred dollars a year per student. We are funding that because this decision was all our own doing. The other day, a person came to the house and said he was a retired chemistry professor and would be glad to help with our home school. All we had to do was ask.

Our decision to do the home-schooling was based on a couple of things. I got concerned when my youngest son was in third grade and was having no success at all in math. He needed one-on-one instruction. I was also concerned with the Native American religious practices they were learning in school. Our family is Baptist, and I don't believe that religion should be taught in school. I will take care of that part of their education.

Education has always been important to me. When I think back on my childhood and teen years, the schools I attended stand out as a very important part of my life. After I was born in Dallas, Texas, my family moved to the Chicago area, where I received my early education. There I attended one of the first magnet schools in the country—the Walt Disney Magnet School. We had a diverse mixture of students, including blacks, whites, Asians, and East Indians. I was one of two Native American students. It was a really good experience, and I enjoyed school.

I had applied to a high school that was very difficult to get into. I was accepted, but then my parents had to move to Tupelo, Mississippi, because of my father's work. I was disappointed, but I was too young to stay behind by myself. In Tupelo I attended Carver Junior High, the only integrated school in the system. It was so different, and I was the only Native American student in the whole school. I didn't feel I belonged in either the Caucasian group or the black group.

And other factors also made it difficult to adjust. For example, the area was very spread out, so we had to drive everywhere. I had a hard time getting used to the Southern accent, which sounded at first like a foreign language to me. And the pace of life was so much slower than what I was used to in Chicago. Of course, there was no snow; everything was the same, and I missed the seasons. I believe we were the only Indian family in that town. Every time we would even go out to our backyard, we could just feel it. It was a very different situation.

    I went up to Ponsford that next summer to visit my sister. I was happy to go; I needed to get away from Tupelo. Soon after that, my dad said that maybe he and my mother should move back home, too. His family is originally from the area where my sister lives. My brother had already moved to this area years ago. So we all ended up back in northern Minnesota. I felt much better then, less isolated, and I had family around me.

    After I graduated from Cass Lake High School, I was accepted at the University of Minnesota in Duluth. I chose this over Bemidji State and the University of North Dakota because I had relatives and friends who were already attending there. It was a nice school, but it was just too big. I wasn't accustomed to class sizes of two hundred to three hundred people, and it didn't work out for me. But I ended up living there for eight years anyway.

    The productive part of the Duluth years was that my children were born there. I basically just existed in Duluth, and my career direction wasn't really set. A nurse's aide job got me thinking about a medical career. Once I decided to switch my major to health education with a biology minor, I finished my degree in three years. When my mind was made up, it wasn't hard to stay focused.

    The next summer I was asked to run the Native American program in Duluth, a six-week summer program. I had been in this program myself as a student, so I knew a lot about it. It was a good opportunity for me right after graduation, and as it turned out, it was a stepping-stone to my next job, which I practically walked into. I was at the office of the Indian Students Services' director, looking for a letter of recommendation, when he asked me if I would be interested in taking a job as coordinator of the Native Americans into Medicine Program. I was at the right place at the right time.

I work with undergraduate students to encourage them into medical or health degrees and then to pursue their training. Our basic goal is to get more doctors out into the field. Studies have shown that Indian people relate better to Indian physicians and nurses and to other health providers who are Native American. Right now, we have about eight hundred Native American doctors nationwide. So I encourage students into sciences and the math courses they will need to prepare for a medical or other health-related profession. I visit schools and disperse the information about the program. I tell the students that after they finish their first two years, they should contact me, and I will help them choose the right field and the right school.

We have a lot of problems with retention. For instance, this year we started out with thirty-one Native Americans into Medicine students in the fall, but by the end of the year, we had only fifteen. Some of the students aren't prepared with the right math and science courses, so they get discouraged. We do offer tutoring and mentoring programs to help with this, but some of them just get overwhelmed. Or some of the students have family problems that cause them to leave. Then there are those who think that seven dollars an hour working at the casino is the way to go; this sounds like big bucks to them. We don't call these students "dropouts"; we call them "stop-outs," because many do eventually come back, as I did after eight years in Duluth. The majority of our students are older than average: it takes many people several years to find their way.

Bemidji State is surrounded by Red Lake, Leech Lake, and White Earth, so we have a rather large Native American population. We have 220 Indian students on campus this year—a big increase over last year.

I'm very interested in the history of our culture, but sometimes I think I learned more about it in the Chicago schools than if I had lived here on the reservation all my life. My mother, for instance, has always been interested in Native American art and its history. She has a large collection now. When she finds a fine piece of beadwork or basketry, for example, we do research on it to learn as much as we can. We attend cultural events and often are asked to do shows at nursing homes, schools, and summer tourist events. My children also learn about their heritage through their school projects. We did our family histories, which took us back to the 1500s in the case of my father's family.

My great-grandfather and my maternal grandfather were from Ireland. I am just as proud of my Irish heritage as I am of my Indian heritage. Sometimes it seems to me that I'm supposed to hide my Caucasian side. When I was a child in school, I told my teacher I was Indian. Because I have red hair and light skin, the teacher said, "No, no, but you can be one for Halloween." To me, heritage is just a biological fact; it's there whether anyone thinks it is or not.

My children are enrolled as White Earth tribal members. We are running into some problems now at school with students who are not enrolled but are "descendants of." This can be very confusing for some of our students, and they really stumble when they find they cannot qualify for grants and other financial help.

I believe that I have had a very broad education—from the streets of Chicago to Tupelo, Mississippi, to Duluth, Bemidji, and the reservation area of northern Minnesota. I have learned a lot. My interests are varied. I even take my sons to wrestling matches. We take field trips, too; we have visited the Minnesota Zoo, the Science Museum, and Valleyfair. And once a summer, my mom, the kids, and I take a four-day weekend trip; a few years ago, we visited the Black Hills.

Our house is large and always full of people. My children invite friends almost every weekend. Holidays are really fun, when my brother arrives with his large family.

My life is very full. Besides our jobs and just day-to-day living, we are interested in many things in this family. I like to go on nature walks; photography and beadwork are also interests of mine. I even made my own jingle dress. And I love to surf the Internet. Sometimes I wish I would have chosen computers as a career. Our whole family is very interested in history; many of our projects center around that. We are kind of the historians for the Pine Point Reservation. We make charts, gather information, and collect pictures.

During the next ten years, I plan to work on a master's degree and possibly a doctorate in educational administration. For my sons' sake, I will stay in this area for this work, so they won't have to be uprooted until their college years. Once the kids are in college, I'll decide what happens next with my career.

Ronda Sargent-Estey
Born: December 30, 1958

Ronda Sargent-Estey spent her preschool years in the Anoka, Minnesota, area, where she lived with her parents and younger brother. When they moved to the reservation, Ronda attended the Nay-tah-waush and Mahnomen schools. Her family valued education, and Ronda graduated from Moorhead State University in 1980 with a degree in education. She has taught language arts in the elementary school at Nay-tah-waush and currently has a classroom of her own in the Mahnomen School District. She describes her educational philosophy as "holistic" and believes this perspective is based on the values of her Native American heritage.

Ronda Sargent-Estey

My parents are both White Earth enrollees. My mother is from the Mississippi band and my father from the Pillager band. They are both from large families and grew up mostly in the Nay-tah-waush area. My mother was the youngest of ten children, and as a child, she was bounced around among the homes of her sisters and brothers. That is why we have not maintained such close ties with her family as with my father's family. Both my brother and I are enrolled at White Earth in the Pillager band.

My dad grew up hearing the Ojibwe language. My grandparents would use it especially when they didn't want us children to know what they were talking about. I'm not sure why we are not fluent in the language, other than that we weren't encouraged to speak it at home or school. Some of the kids in my generation did not want to take an interest in their culture and in their language. I think this is a tragedy, and I'm glad this attitude is changing now.

My brother and I were very close growing up since we were only about ten months apart. I was not given an Indian name, but I am named after two uncles on my father's side, Ron and Dan. In our culture, if you are given an Indian name, it is considered a gift. For example, my husband's grandmother gave our middle son an Indian name. She looked at him when he was born, observed him for a few days, and then a name came to her out of the clear blue, which she gave to him. In some tribes this is a very formal process, and in others it is more casual.

My brother and I enjoyed what I would call an extended family in the "projects" of the Nay-tah-waush area. Two or three houses were built by the government, and we all kind of lived together there. I consider myself lucky because of all the support from my dad's brothers and sisters and their kids. We were very close and still are. All my aunts, uncles, cousins, and some of my closest friends are in my extended family. This is especially good for me because my only brother is a sales manager for General Motors and lives in Michigan. My extended-family members are more like brothers and sisters than distant cousins. They are all welcome any time they want to visit.

Life was pretty active around my house. I always admired my dad for helping people. He was in tribal government, so he was always in the middle of some controversy. I learned from watching this that you can't please everybody all the time. I also learned that I didn't want to have anything to do with politics. The phone was ringing all the time, people were coming to the house, and no matter how hard my father tried, there were always one or two people who were left with negative feelings.

I also watched the changes in women's roles as I was growing up. My mother worked outside the home, but my grandmother didn't. My husband's mom believes the woman should be at home to take care of the kids and the house, but my mom was never like that. I have never felt any restrictions as a woman on the reservation. And I have never thought of myself as having limitations because I'm female. For instance, I'm a volunteer at the fire department, and we are all treated as *firefighters,* not as men and women. But I believe that society still expects women to be the dominant player in household chores and child care.

I have mixed feelings about the impact of the casino on our community. It has certainly helped the economy by bringing in jobs, but I have concerns about people gambling away their money. I think it was too bad that gambling had to be brought to the reservation to provide jobs. I worked there for two and a half years, and I observed how people started taking more pride in themselves and in their work. In this way, it has been good. Both my sons have been employed there, besides going to school.

Education was really a high priority when I was growing up, and my parents were quite strict. Now, with both parents working or with single-parent families, people get so caught up in the business of everything that there is not so much time for the kids. Value systems have changed as parents have become more involved with earning a living.

My own education took place here at the Nay-tah-waush Elementary School, which was 99 percent Native American. Then I went to Mahnomen High School until the eleventh grade, when I dropped out. After being out of high school for a while, I knew I could do more with my life, so I began taking extension courses at White Earth offered by Moorhead State University. I got my GED [graduate equivalency degree] and went on to college. I graduated in education in 1980, and my brother graduated in business in 1989. A number of people encouraged and helped me: my parents, my brother, teachers, and counselors. I drove in to the campus every day. Sometimes my dad came along to help with the driving. I did my student teaching in Waubun and Detroit Lakes.

My father died one week before my graduation. This was really tough. I wanted him to see this happen for me. My mother is still living in the projects of Nay-tah-waush, and this is where I returned to be a teacher. I started with seventy students as the language-arts teacher for kindergarten through third grade. I realized quite soon that what I really wanted was to have my own classroom, where I would have a chance to bond with the class. I am really happy now with my own classroom in Mahnomen.

A few years ago, we were working very hard in the high school to keep track of dropouts and setting up programs to keep kids in school. For a while, we saw improvements. But now I see the problem beginning to happen again. I think the students are searching to belong to some place or some thing. This happens especially if they are not involved in sports or other interests in school or if they do not have a strong support system at home. In school I can see the effects of a stable home where the parents stress the importance of education, as well as the impact of troubled homes, on the behavior of children. There *is* a correlation.

I always think of the student as a whole being—socially, intellectually, and spiritually. I think this belief comes from my heritage. Where I teach now in Mahnomen, there is a mix of Indians and non-Indians. This doesn't concern me; I try to be sensitive to all the students when I present teachings from my culture and heritage.

I have no real staunch religious beliefs, but spirituality is important to me. I remember always going to church with my parents, even in the Cities. When we moved to the reservation, we attended a little neighborhood church. But when Brad and I were married, his dad and mom were ministers so that changed our direction a little, and we ended up going to the Episcopal church.

Some of the values taught in church were the same as those taught in the Indian religion. My immediate family has not been involved in any traditional ceremonies; right before my dad died, he had a very strong belief that we should not take part in the ceremonies. We observed a real peace come upon him and respected his feelings about this.

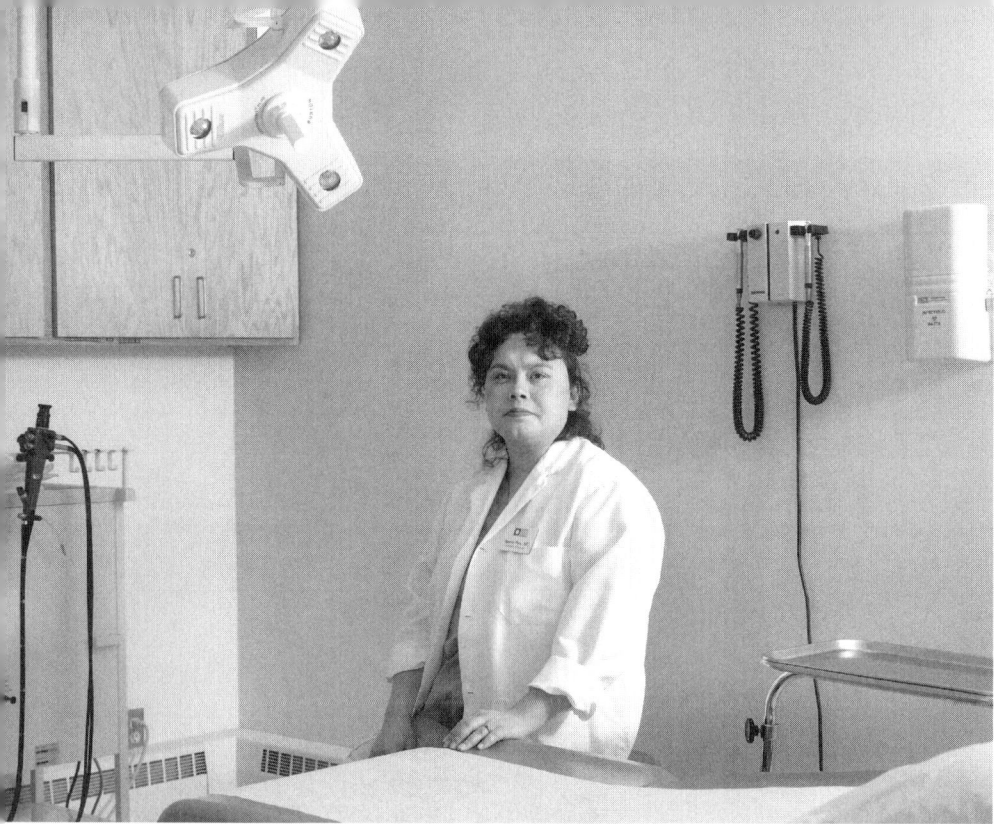

Valerie Fox

Born: February 24, 1968

Valerie Fox has always valued education. She started school at Moorhead State University when her daughter was six weeks old. Valerie pursued courses that would lead to a career in medicine, although she also considered law. She has met and overcome many obstacles while working to achieve her goals. All her life, she has been searching for greater knowledge and understanding of her heritage and ancestry. She and her husband live in Perley, Minnesota.

I have been on this earth for nearly thirty years, and I am still not sure which path I'm on. I can clearly see that school has been a big focus for me. I have always done well in school, but I have had a hard time staying on track. Accounting, medicine, law? I've thought about it all. All I really know for sure is that I want to do something where I can be a mother to my child and work at a job where I help people.

In 1986 I went to Carleton College. Big culture shock! While I was there, I found out I was pregnant, so I had a perfect excuse to leave. Even though I left school then, I did make some decisions before Amy was born. First, I would never live on welfare; second, I would do something to support my child; and, finally, I would move back to Moorhead and live there with Amy and her dad.

I started school at Moorhead State University when Amy was six weeks old. She went to college with me almost every day. She'd attend preschool or sometimes go with me to the chemistry lab. I remember her sitting there in the lab with goggles on while I worked with chemicals.

That first year is really a blur. I had no car, so I rode the bus with my baby. The first day, I was so afraid; I can hardly describe it. I was still breast-feeding. I thought, "What the hell am I doing here?" I didn't even know where the bookstore was. I had money from loans and scholarships, but I didn't know where my classes were or what to do with my baby. I found day care; I found the bookstore; and I got to my first class, English 101. After the small classes at Carleton, I was surprised to see about thirty people in the room. But I started to feel good because, looking around, I guessed they were all as dorky as I was. I thought, "Thank God, I'm going to make it. No one looks any smarter than I am!"

All the way through school, I counted the days and the credits. I just kept plugging along. I went eight quarters straight, with two summer schools. I was told at the beginning of my chemistry course that I should consider dropping out since I hadn't had chem in high school, or calculus either. I stuck it out anyway.

One day the girl who sat next to me asked what I was majoring in. I said, "I don't have a major. I don't even know what I'm doing here." She replied that she was going to be a doctor. I thought, "Ha, you do worse than I do on tests." So

I decided to major in chemistry. I liked it, and it wasn't that hard. Then I really started wondering if I could be a physician.

Meanwhile, my child was getting bigger. My dreams got big, too, so I took my child and went to Mayo Medical School. This was the hardest thing I've ever done. I flunked the first two bio-chem tests I took—not by much, but I flunked. I was discouraged at times. In fact, sometimes I thought I would die. I thought I would get kicked out of med school, but I didn't. I even passed gross anatomy.

I had been at Mayo for a year when my boyfriend, Mike, Amy, and I went to Disney World. It was great fun, but it was then that my life began to fall apart. I was implanted with Norplant on May 7, 1993; within a month, I ended my relationship with Mike, and within two months, I let my daughter go back to her dad because I couldn't deal with the stress of parenting any more. Within four months, I had quit school and became really depressed. My friends would come and look for me in my apartment because I wasn't in school. They thought I might be dead. I wasn't dead really, just watching TV or something in this little basement apartment. It was scary. I called my mom in October of 1993 and told her I was not doing well and needed to quit school. I took a leave, went back to Moorhead, and became a waitress at TJ's Truck Stop. This is where I was after six years of school.

In January 1994, I moved to St. Paul to be nearer my daughter and took a job at the American Indian Learning Research Center at the University of Minnesota. Then I found a different job with the American Indians AIDS Task Force and worked there for about six months. I got fired and ended up back in my parents' home in White Earth. I had a job there for a while, but it didn't work out. In April I was accepted back at medical school at the University of North Dakota, where I completed psychology, pediatrics, and ob/gyn. Considering everything that had led up to this, school actually went very well.

In college, I was probably the happiest I have ever been. I had friends. I worked with the American Indian Association at Moorhead State University. There were more than eighty of us on the campus, much to my surprise. Before this, I didn't even know what being Indian was. All I knew was that it often set me apart. The question was always there: "How important is this Indian thing in knowing who I am?"

My dad still lives in the same house my grandmother lived in. Grandmother was a medicine woman. I think I may be a lot like my grandmother in her beliefs and her spirituality. Because of my education, I also have faith in science. I believe that something controls everything; people and things interact for reasons. I believe I was put here to experience things.

My family has been a support in a way. For example, I see my cousins often. We grew up together. I remember piling into a jeep and going to church, even if it was just to get out of the woods on a Sunday morning. We still get together, sometimes for holidays. These are the people who know my most intimate secrets. They are the people who say, "I would never let you be my doctor! Only if you're the only one available." I laugh, because if they have a medical problem, who do they call? Me.

Sometimes I feel I should go back to Mayo to do a residency in ob/gyn. This is what I want to do. But knowing me, I won't make that choice. Somehow I'm always striving to get away, but I can't. I've joked with some people, saying that what I've really aspired to all my life is to be a white male doctor. That seems to be the way to go.

What I've learned about being Native American and female has been very hit-and-miss. For example, at Riverside Elementary I was teased about being different. They called me a Chink. I said, "If you're going to call me names, at least get the name right!" Other times I was very isolated, like the summers I spent in Mahnomen knowing my father was full-blooded Native American. I guess it's not surprising that I'm still trying to figure out who I am.

One thing I did learn is that it's not easy to be very bright and Indian at the same time. The Indian kids didn't like me answering questions, but the white kids didn't like me no matter how bright I was. One time I wrote an editorial to the *Mahnomen Pioneer* about some of the problems I'd encountered in school involving segregation, integration, and conflict. I received a phone call about the letter, and they basically told me it was none of my business.

I've gone to so many different schools, and each one has had a different racial mix. Fitting in was easy if you drank, smoked cigarettes, and partied. This worked to help me fit in, but because of it, I almost didn't graduate. Many bad things happened in high school. But the academic work was easy. I know I didn't learn as much as I should have.

During my junior year at Moorhead State, I found out there were eighty-eight Native Americans on campus. We started having get-togethers and doing things. During American Indian Awareness Week, we had the tri-college pow-wow. My daughter started dancing at that time, too; she's a jingle-dress dancer. My dad told me that when he was growing up they would go to dances almost every weekend. They weren't big productions like they are now. He has pictures of himself dancing. It sounds like life was just one big powwow.

In college I took some classes to learn more about my heritage. I used to think that if you read it in a book, it must be true. I've given up being real angry about some of the falsehoods I've been taught. When I got the job in St. Paul at the American Indian Learning Research Center, I learned a lot by attending pipe ceremonies, smudges, and powwows. This was really great fun. I'm still interested in teaching the culture to kids so they'll know the real history that I never learned in high school.

I am tired of fighting everything. I am about ready to give up and walk the red road and live right. I think with native people, a lot of them come to that conclusion. It's a way of life I'm talking about. What it requires, in most cases, is sobriety. That's the key to the whole thing. I also know that for me to have strong self-esteem, I must be a mother first, then a physician, then a wife. I went into a depression when I lost these priorities. It's been a struggle to get my life back, and it's hard to keep things together. But it's even harder to get back on track once you've gone astray.

Saraphine Martin is a well-known elder on the reservation. She has seen a great many changes in her lifetime, and some of these distress her. Saraphine and her husband are active church members involved in community work. She likes to keep busy and fills her days helping others and pursuing her hobby of basketry. Saraphine came from a large family, but only three of her siblings are still living.

Saraphine Martin
Born: September 15, 1918

Saraphine Martin

I attended the government school at Hayward, Wisconsin, for three years, starting there when I was just seven or eight years old. One day I was sitting by a lake on a hillside, talking to my friend. We were talking in our native language, and someone must have heard us. We got a strapping when we got back to the school. I had wanted to go to this school because I had a cousin who was going there, so my mother signed me up for a three-year term. After three years at this school, I couldn't understand my mother speaking Indian when I got home, even though I could still speak a little. My grandfather also spoke the language, and I spent a lot of time with his family. He told us many stories about what happened a long time ago. It was interesting to me, and it helped me get some of my language back. My grandfather's name was Wolf Rock. He was a strong Catholic and wanted me to be baptized in a Catholic church.

When I returned from boarding school, I attended Pine Point School until the ninth grade. When I quit school, I worked for the NYA, the National Youth Administration, for a while. I did everything there, outside and inside work. Sometimes I helped the cooks at the school. While I was living in my grandfather's house, I got to know his second wife very well. She didn't have any hands. She told me she got cold and lost her hands. She taught me so much. She used to cook and make raised bread. She did everything. I was surprised. She could even sew and thread her own needle. I would ask her how she did that, and she would show me. I learned cooking, ricing, and how to make maple syrup from my mother and grandmother, and I heard stories from my grandfather. I have tried to pass these stories on to my children and foster children.

I was a Catholic growing up, and when I came back to Ponsford, I went to catechism to be confirmed. I attended with my first cousin. We used to go there every day to get prepared. When we were ready to be confirmed, we were all in a line. When it was my turn, they asked me what my name was. "You don't belong here," they said, and pushed me aside. I didn't know what to feel. I was about sixteen years old. I ran all the way home, went to my room, and stayed there for two weeks. I didn't eat anything, just a cup of tea. My mother kept asking me, "What's the matter?" I wouldn't tell her. I just kept quiet. After about three weeks, I said to her, "I'm real ashamed, and that's why I haven't told you anything. I'm going to tell you now." I told her what happened. She said, "Well, if you want to quit going, there's another church on the other side of town." So I started going to church there, and they noticed me. We started having prayer meetings at our home. I asked my mother to tell them I wanted to join this church. The priest talked to me after church that Sunday. He said, "You'll have to be received by the bishop. You come." I've been there ever since.

I've never been very involved in traditional ceremonies. My mother danced; she had a jingle dress and everything. And one of my sisters, the one who teaches the Ojibwe language at the school in Ponsford, dances now.

In 1945 I started living with a man whose wife had left him. He had one son. One day I found his boy standing by the creek. A bunch of kids were swimming around and playing, but he was just standing there, lonely. I called to him and asked him to get in the car, but he wouldn't. I went home and got his dad and when we returned, we still had a hard time getting him into the car. He was full of lice, and his clothes were just rags. We cleaned him up, and he stayed with us until he joined the army at eighteen. He eventually called me Mom. He married a girl from Red Lake, and they had three daughters. The youngest lives right near here. We also raised my niece's two daughters. When the girls were about three or four, my niece asked me if I could watch the girls for a couple hours. A couple hours became two weeks, and the courts finally gave us custody. Both girls have graduated from high school.

I do the cooking at the community center. We serve anybody who wants to come. We deliver about fifteen trays a day, and about twelve people come into the center. I've learned quite a bit about nutrition working there. My mother died from diabetes, and I think diet is partly to blame. I don't think our people had this problem when they were eating more wild berries, grains, and other wild foods.

I think a lot that happens today is related to drugs and alcohol. Things get stolen and broken, and the old people don't get as much respect as they used to. But my husband and I stay very busy. He is eighty-one years old and the bell ringer at the

Saraphine Martin

church. Many people come to visit us, and I still make baskets when I can get the materials. People laugh at me when I say I have more white friends than Indian friends. They ask me why this is, and I tell them that they talk to me and I talk back. It just happens. My husband is the same way. We believe God made all people equal. White people are made just like we are. And that's the way it is.

Juanita Blackhawk
Born: July 15, 1954

Juanita Blackhawk is a traditional quillwork artist whose work can be seen all over the United States and in Europe; recently a piece of her work was displayed in Peru. Juanita's father was of Norwegian heritage, and her mother was almost full-blooded Anishinabe from White Earth. She has always considered White Earth her home, even though she grew up in many different places, including the state of Washington, Los Angeles, and several towns in Minnesota. Juanita has experienced many traumatic situations in her life, but she has survived—as an artist, a political activist, a wife, and a parent to two of her nephews. Juanita placed her only biological child, a son, with adoptive parents when he was born; she still has contact with him.

My mother was an alcoholic. She and my father were divorced when I was about three-and-a-half. Daddy got custody of four of us, but Social Services came in and convinced him that it was better for us kids to be in a family situation. My sister and I were placed in different homes in Halstead, Minnesota. I saw her at school, but I was not allowed to acknowledge her as my sister. Another brother and sister were placed in Borup, Minnesota, and I had very little contact with them. It was rough growing up. My sister and I were the only Indians in an all-white school, and I fought almost every day of my life. I would pick the biggest boy and take him down and start blasting him. I was suspended from school at least once in each grade until we moved out to the West Coast.

I was formally adopted shortly after my fourth birthday. But I knew my whole biological family and where they lived. I never forgot about them. I left my adoptive home when I was fifteen, a victim of childhood sexual abuse that started shortly after I was adopted and continued until I left. At age thirty-seven or thirty-eight, I began to remember what had happened to me as a child, and it almost drove me crazy. I realized I had been a virtual slave in that house, a live-in servant. My adoptive parents were middle-upper class in the community. Not everyone knows what goes on behind closed doors. I made peace with my adoptive mother, but I took my adoptive father to court in a civil suit.

This was a very hard time for me. I went back to Halstad to see Daddy and my sister Marcie. My adoptive father had started rumors all over town about me. Daddy and Marcie supported me in facing this. I finally did receive some apologies from some of the people. My adoptive parents moved when the town realized that my adoptive father had lied. And I went back to Washington to the home of my foster parents.

I love my foster parents dearly. Without them I wouldn't be here today. All this time I was very screwed up. I was using alcohol and drugs and had a lot of trouble with relationships. Jim and Gina, my foster parents, had a lot of understanding about the problems I was facing. They were friends to me more than parents, but they still had the authority I needed and respected. I was torn between home in White Earth and my foster parents in Washington. After 1972, when Daddy died, I went back and forth, trying to find my way. I would spend a couple years in Minnesota and then go back, because I missed both places.

I finally decided I had to go home and stay there to find out who I really was. I had been on a downhill slide, and I was killing myself. I knew I had to get away. I returned to Minnesota, but I still bounced around—Minneapolis, Ponsford, Red Lake, and Cass Lake; wherever my sisters, brother, aunts, and uncles were, that's where I would stay.

I had been told a lot of lies about my mother and father by my adoptive parents, especially by my adoptive father. I wanted to find my mother and clear up the stories, so I made plans to go to Cutbank, Montana, where my mother had been living. I was excited; I knew it was something I had to do. But then I found out my mother had died. I hadn't seen her since the divorce, and I was furious that this didn't work out for me. My dad died in 1972, so there were more years of going back and forth. I was in Washington when Mount St. Helens erupted, and I heard that my grandpa was sick. I wanted to go home then but I was delayed, and he died before I got home. I was in L.A. when I decided to go home to Minnesota. I gave away everything I had, except the clothes on my back, and jumped on a plane for Minneapolis. I stayed with my brother then for about a year and a half. Sometime later I met Charles again, a man I had known several years earlier. We were married at a traditional Anishinabe ceremony in my mother-in-law's home with all our family around us.

The traditional ceremony had much more meaning for us than a civil one would have. I had been taken to church from the time I was four, all different churches, and it was very confusing. But I knew a lot of the traditional ways because my grandpa was Midewiwin, which is our grand medicine society, our traditional religion. This meant more to me and has stayed with me until this day. I have a lot of good memories of Grandpa and funny stories to tell. I always counted on him being on the "res" when I was a kid. My sister and I brought Grandpa to St. Paul to live with us for a while, and we had times that I will never forget. Sometimes Grandpa would get mad at us because we couldn't understand him when he would talk to us in Ojibwe. He was always playing practical jokes, and he wore a headband all the time to keep his eyes open. He made us laugh! And I remember that I was always his girl. I would sit on the floor with my head on his knee, and he would stroke my hair and tell us stories, old, old traditional stories, cultural things. He was an anchor in my life.

I'm not sure exactly when it happened, but I started using more traditional Anishinabe ways. I believe this helped me become sober and quit drugs. When I came back home in 1984 or 1985, I started to learn more about my heritage and religion. My sister was living with a medicine man, a spiritual leader, and my brother had also gone back to the traditional ways because of what he had learned through AIS [American Indian Services]. So it was very easy for me to get back into it while living with them. I learned the daily rituals of the traditional way of life. I knew this was the only way I could remain sober and straight, alcohol- and drug-free, so I left the Minneapolis area and moved up north.

In June 1991 I met a person who taught me how to do quillwork. This art form became the real catalyst for my staying sober. At this time I began remembering the abuse in my childhood, and I started therapy. One day a medicine man spoke to one of the classes I was taking at Bemidji State University. He helped me with some healing rituals and gave me my Anishinabe name and my spirit colors. Everybody has colors, spirits that protect and guide them, but they are all different colors. The naming and the spirit colors are similar in a way to being baptized. You go back to the Great Spirit and Earth Mother.

Our language was never written down to preserve the history of our traditions. We have had to rely on oral communication. That's why I am studying the Ojibwe language. Once I become fluent, I will probably be initiated back into the Midewiwin society.

The people of Red Lake are more traditional than the other reservations are. But many of us have a renewed interest now and are going back. We are giving up drinking and drugs because that isn't part of our history, just as swearing is not. In the original Ojibwe language, there were no cuss words and there is no word for goodbye. We always say giga-wabi-min, which means "We will see you."

Over the past twenty years, I have been involved and interested in politics. I have been outspoken when it comes to my heritage as an American Indian. (I hate using that term. I'm Anishinabe.) I fought and defended my heritage almost every day when I was growing up. In the schools I attended, the students were mostly black or white; I wasn't either, so I was shunned by both. I went to many different schools and ended up in the tenth grade with only one or two credits needed for graduation. I took some classes at Tacoma Community College in Washington and completed some correspondence courses. One day I was downtown in St. Paul and saw a sign for GED [graduate equivalency degree] testing. I walked in, took the test, and got my GED. Later, when I attended the University of Minnesota, I worked with the Office of Minority and Special Student Affairs, the Native American Center, and the American Association of Indian Students. I have always been interested in truth in education. I was on the school board at Pine Point School for a while. There were efforts to do away with traditional culture classes or anything that was traditionally Native American. I fought this. We have made some progress, but there is still work to be done.

My work now is primarily in the art field. There is so much talent here on the reservation, but it's not getting out to the public. I would like to start an association to help artists market their work and to educate the public. This is a very slow process because the artists don't trust the public any more. They have been taken advantage of too many times, and people who are not Native American have also duplicated their work.

My family is very significant to me now. My sister, my nieces and nephews, and now their own children are such a big part of my life. I missed out on so much when I was growing up. It means everything to me to be connected with all of them again.

Lorraine Faye Lindsay

Born: November 10, 1950

Lorraine Lindsay is the married mother of one son. Her faith in God is very important to her. She has been active in the ownership and management of small businesses, and she is constantly seeking ways to express her compassion by helping others.

I was raised on the White Earth Reservation and attended two little country schools just north of Ogema, Minnesota. There were seven sisters and two brothers in my family. My mother stayed home with us until we were all in school. My father was a car salesman and mechanic. My school memories of those early years are quite pleasant. There were two teachers for the students, who were divided into two groups. I remember the most fun was being able to help the teacher erase the blackboards and to work in the library. I went to the Detroit Lakes Schools for the secondary grades and graduated from high school there.

I was eighteen when I married my husband. We had gone to the same schools and had similar interests. We both wanted to live a peaceful Christian life, so we headed for Florida looking for this way of life. But we didn't find it there, and in a roundabout way, we ended up in Pennsylvania as caretakers at a Christian camp called Blue Mountain Retreat. We stayed on staff there for six years. Even though we enjoyed living in Pennsylvania, we were really lonesome for our families back in Minnesota. Also, my husband took a bad fall from scaffolding while working in the gymnasium and broke several bones. Everything kind of brought us back to Minnesota in 1985. We're a pretty tight-knit family, and all of us are now living within a twenty-mile radius.

While growing up, my parents were pretty distant. We didn't hear "I love you." There was a lot of emotional emptiness in our household. I can see how this has affected my siblings, mainly my sisters. They don't cry about it, but I know it bothers them and has influenced the choices they've made in their adult lives. I'm bothered by it, too. I handle it by just crying or letting it go. I think my dad never communicated with us in a positive way because he was too busy working. One day recently, I went over to my parents' home with a notebook and had them tell me their entire life stories. I had a need to find out about their lives before they died. I took down the details of where they've been and what they've done, trying to discover who they really are. I want to put together a little album of our family's history.

We were living in Pennsylvania when we adopted our only child as an infant. In raising our son, we've become very aware of the breakdown of Christian family values. We see the dangers in not committing to discipline or not going to church on Sundays. We try to train our child in the way he should go. Building his self-esteem is very important to us. I'm sure this is due to my own childhood and upbringing, where self-esteem was not a real consideration. I'd like to see the entire Native American culture be more aware of the consequences of low self-esteem in our youth. I believe it is a part of alcoholism, incest, sexual immorality, and other troubles in our culture. I'd like to see our entire culture brought to a higher level through better education. We need to be proud of our heritage.

Oddly enough, we never talked about being Indian or Native American while growing up. I've never even attended a powwow. We grew up very poor on the reservation. I am very light skinned and don't look Indian, but my two sisters are very dark skinned. They've made comments like "You don't look Indian. You don't have people looking down on you because of your skin color." Actually, when we went out in public, I did have that feeling, but I don't know if it came from being Indian or from being so poor and living on the reservation.

Of the nine of us kids, I'm the only one who has lived out of state. I'm also the only one to own my own business. You could probably say I'm the adventurous one. I've worked at the Christian retreat, at a turkey plant, and as a receptionist and a waitress. I received a diploma in small-business management from the Detroit Lakes vocational school. After my son was in school, I bought the café in Callaway and ran it for about a year and a half. We remodeled and totally fixed it up. During my ownership, the business tripled. I think I thrive on a challenge. I like to prove to myself and to my dad that I can do things. I sold the café to one of the waitresses, and she's still there.

I've always been involved in sales, and I love it. I like sales positions where people come to me with their needs, rather than my going to them; it's much easier to sell that way. After selling the café, I was offered a position in Mahnomen at the Women's Business Center. It was a three-year demonstration project to help women start their own businesses. I was a small-business-development specialist. While there, I worked really hard. I did business plans, met with clients, and ran training classes. I let Indian women know they could start their own businesses if they really wanted to.

After leaving the Women's Business Center, I started up a small business with my sister-in-law, Juanita Lindsay. She has very strong marketing skills, and we went through the small-business-management course together. I knew we'd make a good team. One day she came over with a product idea: jerky-juice meat marinade. The tribal council licensed us, and a U.S. Department of Health employee came out and inspected my kitchen. Within two weeks, we were bottling our meat marinade. I found out where we could obtain the bottles, and I knew where to order the ingredients through my inventory work at the café. With my background, starting a new business was nothing foreign. The business has slowed down a bit since my sister-in-law's back surgery, but we're continuing with our marketing. My son helps with bottling during the summer.

I was raised Catholic, a very poor Catholic. We went to church on Christmas and Easter. I've always had a lot of religious conviction in my heart, though. I can remember getting up and begging my mom to take us to church on Sundays. I was always searching for something. I feel the Lord has been working with me my whole life. I've recently begun evaluating the importance of material things in my life and realize they mean nothing compared with how we can help others. There are so many hurting people. My prayer is: "God, I want to help make a difference." I don't care if I live in an old tarpaper shack. While working at the Blue Mountain Retreat, I saw how they ran a free-clothing business for the needy called Operation Blessing. People in the community could come in and take whatever they needed. Everything was clean and well-organized. I would like to set up something like that here on the reservation. I'd like to see us take care of our own. As it stands now, people in need have to go into Detroit Lakes for furniture, clothing, food, and so on. I'd like to have one building right here where people could go.

I feel very in tune with people's lives and hurts because of what I've gone through in my own childhood and adult life. Our marriage has had some rocky times, partly due to my drinking. Considering my past lifestyle, I thank God that I'm still alive today. Our pastor recently told us that because of what we've been through in our marriage, my husband and I could counsel other married couples with similar problems. I believe that if this is how I can serve, those doors will open for me.

Angelique Stevens is a student at Bagley High School. She lives with her parents, her older brother, and two younger sisters. Angelique is experiencing some typical adolescent conflicts at home as she asserts her independence. She is also having difficulty finding the right outlet for expressing her many interests. Her perspective on life reflects all the developmental issues that teenagers encounter, as well as those experienced only by Native American teenagers. Typically, she is unsure but optimistic about her future plans. Angelique's many friends, both Native American and white, are very important to her.

Angelique Marie Stevens
Born: March 10, 1983

I live in Rice Lake with my family and go to school in Bagley, Minnesota, about twenty minutes away. My father works construction, and my mother is a school counselor. I have two little sisters, Marissa and Stacey. I think our relationship is pretty normal. I love them and all that, but sometimes we have fights, both physical and verbal. These fights happen when my sisters get crabby.

When I think about school, I think about my friends, the subjects I like, and the trouble I get into for being tardy. It seems to me that the subjects are okay, but the teachers give me problems. The assistant principal is upset with me because I can't get to a couple of classes on time. He wants me to plan better and has given me some suggestions, which might work, but I always forget.

I think math is my favorite subject. I am in geometry right now, and I like that. We get some computer time, too; that's interesting, but we can only use the Internet if we have a signed permission slip. What I find boring about school is that we have ninety-minute classes, and a lot of that time we just have to sit and listen to teachers. We also have closed lunch periods. We would be better off if we had a break to leave at noon. I guess they think we are going to skip school or something if they let us go. We have to stay in school all day, just like a prison.

I also have some trouble in school because I am kind of loud sometimes. Like one day in class we were discussing voting. Do we have a *duty* to vote or a *right* to vote? I was on the right-to-vote side, and we were all yelling at each other across the room. I don't think we should *have* to vote if we don't want to. Making up my own mind is important to me.

Some of my friends think there is prejudice in the school. The other day my cousin was wearing a cheerleader jacket. One of the teachers called the principal because she thought my cousin was holding a gun inside her jacket. The principal and some teachers came down and made her empty her pockets slowly. She pulled out some Hershey Kisses. I guess they felt dumb about that. A white girl also was wearing a cheerleader jacket and had the same things inside her pocket, but no one said anything about that. The teacher apologized to her, but my cousin was almost crying and is now thinking about going to the Circle of Life School.

We used to have an Amerind Club at our school. One of the advisors said that it's against the law to have one-race clubs. Now we are discussing having white kids, too, and changing the name. I don't see the point of this because it won't be an Amerind Club anymore. Amerind stands for American Indian.

I have a lot of white friends, and I get along with most of them most of the time. There was one week, though, when I had two "harassments" filed against me. Two kids said I wanted to beat them up, but I hadn't even talked to them. I don't understand this. I think sometimes it must be the way I look that makes people afraid of me.

When I get home from school, I have to watch my little sisters. They have two dogs. I have to watch out for my youngest sister on the school bus, too, to see that nobody tries to fight with her or anything. Stacey is only eight, so she needs someone to watch out for her. My other sister and I just watch out for her all the time.

My mom and dad get home after we do, so I usually do some cleaning up after school. I do straightening, sweeping, and putting things in order. We have to do this, or we can't go out at night or do anything. Sometimes I think I do most of the work around here.

My Grandpa Bert and my Grandma Lucy live just two houses down from us. Grandpa works on cars, and Grandma is a grandma. These are my dad's parents, and I see them often.

My brother is in the eleventh grade. He and I belong to the White Earth Reservation Youth Council. My brother is the treasurer. We have both held offices in the council. The purpose of the council is to help out the youth in our area. We go to meetings almost every Wednesday and plan events. Right now we are planning a powwow for right after New Year's Eve. We hope the council can provide enough fun and worthwhile activities to keep the kids interested. The officers and representatives have to present positive role models. Sometimes it is hard to always be expected to make good decisions, but I think it's worth it.

Last summer we went to Arizona for a unity meeting. The people who went were representatives of the big White Earth Council. The trip was amazing to me. We saw things we hadn't dreamed of because we were from the woods. We saw a prostitute who wasn't even a girl. There were so many of us there, about two thousand. We visited reservations like Gila Bend. We met people from the Navajo and Apache bands. We were there for about four days, meeting people from many states: New York, Mississippi, California, New Mexico, Minnesota, South Dakota, North Dakota, and Montana. We stopped in Colorado, where there was an outdoor Jacuzzi. We went through Wyoming and then stopped in Oklahoma, where the bombing had taken place. It was a very good trip. We had the usual problems, I guess, but it was a success. I learned a lot.

I like to be involved with social things. Yesterday I decorated for a dance that our youth council sponsored. There's a van that goes around Rice Lake and takes people where they need to go; about twenty of us rode this van to the dance. It's a little complicated because the bus has to deliver the Long Lost Lakers and the Rice Lakers. It takes a long time to get us all home. But we had a good time, and I saw a lot of people I hadn't seen for a while. It was a long day, but fun.

Last year I joined basketball, but they hardly let me play. So one day I quit: I walked out in the middle of a game. I didn't walk off the floor, because I never was allowed to play, but I just quit. The reason I think the coach was mad at me was because I forgot a practice. I thought that other girls missed practice once in a while, and they didn't have a problem. Why did I?

When I get mad, I have a temper. Sometimes I lose control and I'm sorry for that. Like last year I got mad at my cousins for hanging around a girl I didn't like. Now we aren't friends anymore. They think I am going to beat them up or something.

Right now I am in a spot where I don't believe in God or the Great Spirit or anything. I am wondering and searching. My parents and I often do not agree on things. My parents told me that I reached a point in my life when I became outspoken. I used to be real shy, but then I became demanding. I want them to know how I feel about my friends, and it seems to me they can't understand. Right now my mother is very mad at me because I have gotten three ISSs [in-school suspensions]. I have to stay after school from three to five o'clock. I got these for being tardy. My mother thinks I am too outspoken: I say what I think, and I say it loudly sometimes. I have a lot of opinions about school codes, school rules, and school policies. And I speak out—which gets me into trouble. I'm afraid this is my nature, and I will always be this way.

Erma Vizenor
Born: October 5, 1944

Erma Vizenor grew up on and around the White Earth Reservation, where she learned the traditional ways of her Native American culture. Her educational experience started with one-room schoolhouses and ended in a doctoral program at Harvard. Her career in education included being both a teacher and an administrator. She is most well-known, however, as a political activist and reformer. Erma has had a full family life as a devoted wife and mother. Since her husband died in 1998, she has spent some time assessing her life and deciding where her work and interests will lead her. She lives in the country near White Earth, and intends to complete her work on constitutional reform before moving on to something else. She never plans to retire, but will go on working in some capacity to accomplish the changes she considers necessary for her people.

I am a very spiritual person. I couldn't breathe one moment without my spiritual connection to God. This is my source of strength. I believe it comes from my heritage, growing up with my parents, three brothers, and three sisters in the Pine Point area on the reservation. My mother was only sixteen when I was born. She and my father had just finished the wild-rice harvest at Rice Lake when she was taken to the Indian hospital in Cass Lake, where I was born.

I believe we had a very stable family life, but we moved around a great deal so my father could work. Our family moved with the seasons, harvesting rice in August and September and then moving to the Red River Valley to pick potatoes, top onions, and pick carrots and cabbage. Of course, this meant we would miss a lot of school and change schools frequently. I finished the sixth grade when I was twelve.

It had always been a dream of mine to be a doctor. When one of us kids was sick, we very seldom were seen by a doctor. So I pictured myself growing up and becoming a pediatrician. My auntie in Los Angeles was a nurse, and she had promised to come and get me when I finished the sixth grade and take me to L.A. to go to school. She came and we left, riding a Greyhound bus through Canada and down the West Coast to Los Angeles. She sent me to a parochial school, a day academy. It was a small, very good school, and with the help of the tutoring I got from my aunt, I was able to make up for the gaps in my education.

I did well in school, and I am very grateful to my aunt for giving me this opportunity. But when I heard the train whistle at night I would get lonesome and want to go home. After three years, I finished up the ninth grade and left for home. I think my aunt was disappointed in me. I found high school very hard back home, with the lifestyle my family was leading. I attended five different high schools in one year, and I finally dropped out. I was miserable. I called my auntie, and she took me back for my tenth-grade year at the academy. When I returned home this time, I stayed with my mother's relatives and attended school in Park Rapids. This is when I met Dallas. He became the love of my life. We helped each other get through school, and we were very, very proud of ourselves when we made it through graduation. We got married right away and soon became parents. Being an educator and looking back at all the obstacles, I think it's kind of a miracle that we made it through school.

We spent a year or so in Minneapolis with our daughter Jody and then returned to the reservation. Both Dallas and I went to vocational school and took two-year courses. I was working as a records clerk for the Head Start program when I saw an ad about a college program, Project Equality. My boss really encouraged me to go for it. My sister and brother and I were admitted through this program, and the next year my husband came also. We had to deal with a lot of commuting, but by the end of my first year, I was on the dean's list. I also had another baby during my junior year. It wasn't easy, but we made it through by just helping each other. I graduated in 1972 and enrolled in the graduate program for counseling, which I completed in 1973.

Dallas and I taught at Pine Point then for eight or nine years. In 1981, the state legislature turned the governance of the school over to the tribal government and council. The people at the school had a vision and the education to really take some steps for betterment and were in some ways a threat to the status quo. I wasn't surprised when they fired all of us.

I tried law school for two years at the University of Minnesota, but I really don't think my heart was in it. So I went home and was hired as an elementary teacher at Circle of Life School. I taught grades one through three, and became very interested in the Native American culture. The parents came in and helped with programs involving traditional ceremonies. I started taking night courses at North Dakota State University while I was teaching, and the following year I was hired as a school administrator at the Pine Point School. After about three years, I finished a specialist's degree for school administration.

About that time, I was awarded a Bush Fellowship that I had previously applied for and decided to use it to further my education at Harvard. In April I took my youngest daughter, Chris, and went to Cambridge, Massachusetts, to look over the School of Education at Harvard. I wrote my letter of application while we were there, submitted it, and returned home. By the middle of May, I heard that I had been admitted to the doctoral program in education. I think the fact that I was Native American helped me get in. So I planned to go out east and take Chris, who was a senior that year, with me. She didn't want to leave home but I said she had to come with me and if she didn't like it, she could come back and stay with my husband. It turned out that she liked it very much and finished high school out there. It was a very positive experience for us.

I finished my coursework and research and returned home to write my proposal and dissertation. But then a group of people asked me to be their spokesperson to protest the corruption in government at White Earth. We drafted a statement that I read at a press conference. Then I was into it! I let my dissertation sit on the shelf for five years while I led the movement in White Earth. It was a peaceful movement, but I did spend one whole summer in jail. I traveled throughout the country, telling our story about our fraudulent elections and what kind of corruption we had in government and how the people were suffering. I went to Louisiana, Chicago, all over the East Coast, Washington. They would send me a ticket and I'd go. I met many times with the FBI.

All this time, I was having difficulty writing my proposal for my dissertation. After about five attempts, I just decided I had to go back to be nearer my advisor and my committee. I stayed at a Catholic convent with a friend of mine who is a nun. It was an ideal place to study and work, and by December my proposal was accepted.

I came back home to write my dissertation and from then on, it was just hard work. I'd take my blanket and pillow down into my little office and just write until I was tired. I bought a fax machine so I could work closely with my committee at Harvard. I sat at the computer, and with the help of my husband at the photocopy machine, we got all the drafts together and mailed them in a big box by Federal Express to Harvard. My whole family went east for graduation. It was very exciting!

A doctor who visited our school once a week at Pine Point told me one day that I was a puzzle to him. He said that according to all the statistics, I should have fallen through the cracks. I told him that I've had some significant people in my life who have inspired me. As small as my dreams were, these people made them big dreams and encouraged me to believe in them. My parents, as poor as they were, my auntie, and many others helped me to believe that all I had to do was go to school and study hard, and nothing would be impossible if I set my mind to it. I've always believed that everything can be made better if we work at it. Even as a small child, I was a responsible person. I've had a lot of failures, but it was the successes that meant the most to me, even the small ones. The plan is always the same when I confront a problem: you look at what happened yesterday, decide what you want to have happen tomorrow, and then do what you can do today.

The story of the recent elections is very complicated. What motivated me to be involved was my belief that we must stand together and unite if we are going to be strong. We must avoid the factions that oppose each other and can become volatile. Violence is unacceptable. Our offense was to make injustice visible. My theme was always to unite the tribe and to serve *all* our members, no matter where they are.

Not long ago, my husband said to me, "You don't have to do this. We can move, and you can do whatever you want to do." I thought a while and said, "No, I have to do this. I wouldn't be satisfied unless I had done everything I can with this." My husband didn't like to see me stressed, but that's the way it was. We both knew there was a fight ahead, and I knew he would stand by me. Dallas passed away that evening.

This has been the most discouraging time of my life. Losing my husband has been a terrible experience. All my life, I thought I could take on anything, but I always had him with me. My brother stays with me now, but I feel kind of alone in my house in the woods. I think I'm ready to take some time off to sort things out. I will just tie up what I'm doing with the constitutional reform, and then I will make some plans for the next chapter in my life.

Janet Gordon-Roy is a social worker who places foster children. She works for Human Service Associates, a private family agency in St. Paul that specializes in foster care for youth, both Native American and non-Indian. In 1994 the association worked to establish a Rites of Passage Native American Home in Bemidji for young Indian girls who don't know about their culture and who are dealing with issues of abuse (physical, sexual, and emotional), their own sexuality, and chemical dependency. She returned to school when she was forty years old to receive her credentials for her present career. Before that, Janet was a clerk/typist, a bartender, a cocktail waitress, a dental assistant, and a hairdresser. She received a bachelor's degree from Augsburg College in sociology, with a minor in psychology and a concentration in the study of chemical dependency. She plans to return to Augsburg in the future to receive her master's in social work, and hopes to do career counseling in a school before she retires.

Janet Sara Gordon-Roy
Born: June 28, 1944

Janet Sara Gordon-Roy

I was born in Bagley, Minnesota, and raised in that area until I graduated from high school. There were nine children and my mom and dad. We were very poor. I'd be willing to say that we were a dysfunctional family—lots of alcohol, alcoholism, parties, and things like that. It seemed to me that I was always the one who had to take care of them and fix up things. I don't have many fond memories of being young. I really don't remember being a child. I still have a tendency to take over and do things for people; that's my nature, and I have to watch myself so I don't get too involved in fixing other people's lives.

I went to a one-room country school. We had our milk and lunch downstairs, but most of the time was spent upstairs with a teacher who was a real model for me. She really stays in my mind. She always smelled so good, and she always had a handkerchief. Her name was Jennie Mae Bishop, and she made me eager to learn. Miss Bishop always told me how well I did and how pretty I was. I guess I didn't get too much of that at home. So I did well in school; I was a good student because I wanted to please her.

I ran into some problems, though, when I went to Mahnomen for high school. I found more prejudice there, and, of course, I became interested in boys. Studying became less important. I ran away from home when I was about thirteen, and became a ward of the state. I was called an incorrigible child, but actually I think all I wanted was to be loved. It's painful today to remember this. Now I'm in midlife, and I'm working through a lot of things that troubled me in the past. Besides my personal issues, there are many things connected with my job as a social worker that are not easy to deal with. I have a lot of things going on in my life.

My job involves placing children in foster homes. About half the children I work with are Native American. There are many different types of placements, but our specialty is foster placement for youth. The Indian Child Welfare Act, which was passed about twenty years ago, has caused a lot of changes in the system that places children. It can get to be very confusing because blood-quantum issues become involved. Many of our judges and lawyers do not know enough about the act to follow it accurately. Some placements can end up a real mess. If I could put all this stuff together with my own experiences, I could write a book that would be a number-one best seller.

I understand the importance of a secure family environment when a child is growing up because of my own childhood. I married right out of high school, and my husband and I started our drinking years together. We both went through treatment in the early eighties and have been sober ever since. Life is very different now because we feel everything. We aren't medicated any more.

I have had so many different jobs in my life. It is interesting to look back at all this: the schools I attended, the people who influenced me, and how I ended up in social work. For instance, my probation officer when I was young and "incorrigible" was wonderful. What impressed me most about my teacher in elementary school and my probation officer is that both of them were soft-spoken, really clean, and smart. And that is what I wanted to be; I knew I wanted to be like them in those ways. I probably will finish my career working in a school setting. I know I will always work in one job or another.

The only member of my family whom I have much contact with today is one of my brothers. He is doing very well and is successful in many ways. But I also have some positive things that I enjoy with my other brothers and sisters. We live fairly close to each other and have contact occasionally. I was grateful that I had two full years with my mother before she died; a lot of healing took place. I cleared up some issues from the early days and told her what I would liked to have had from her when I was a child. The sad thing about this is that I see myself doing some of the same things she did, and this is so hurtful. As hard as I try, I still catch myself being the way Mom was.

I always loved my dad and saw him as a kind, gentle person. But then the question arose if he were really my father. I've wondered if my mom was harsh and mean to me over the years because I was a reminder, a constant reminder, of a very difficult part of her life. I can understand this today, but it was hard when I was younger, and it hurt a lot.

My husband says that I was always different from the rest of the family, that I was never satisfied. He says that I had ambition, and he always knew that someday I would go back to school. I know we were very poor—not starving (we always had enough food), but we didn't have the things other people had. My father worked all the time—picked potatoes, lumbered in the woods, peeled pulp—but there was never enough.

When I was growing up, even though we were enrolled at White Earth in the Mississippi band, we were told not to admit that we were Indian. I don't think this was because my parents were ashamed, but back in those days, it was tough. My parents couldn't vote, for example. Everything they did was only because the non-Indian people said they could do it. I sensed the anger about this. There is Chippewa, Irish, and, I believe, Scottish in my background. I think all this "quantum" stuff is nonsense. The way I see it is that people can have an "Indian heart" whether they have bloodlines or not.

I have been given two Indian names. At birth I was named after my mother's mother, a name that means "water drum woman." My pipe carrier friend, who received it from a woman who had watched over me while I was growing up, recently gave the other name to me; it means "pushing the wind woman."

I really figured out who I was, what I was, and what I wanted to become when I went back to school. It has given me a drive and some real pain at times to find out these things about myself. I had to look at my heritage and my early religious experiences to understand who I am today. I studied Chippewa in college and realized that it is a very difficult language. We used to hear it at home once in a while as children, but unless you use it on a daily basis, you won't retain it. My religious instruction as a child was Episcopalian, but when I married, I became Catholic. However, I brought my cultural and traditional beliefs into that. I do believe in one God, a God who is the same for everyone. I talk to my creator every day, and I do not see him as the God I grew up with, who would punish me or come to get me if I did not do the right thing. This background has left me with a lot of strong opinions, and I don't hesitate to state them or to disagree with people. My second given Indian name probably suits me well: "pushing the wind woman."

I think I have come to my spiritual place because of everything that has happened to me. That is why I feel strongly about setting my own path. I often have questions about rules and such that are handed down from the church or through the traditions, and I don't hesitate to ask.

My husband and I attend, and sometimes participate in, the powwows. I see my friend who is a pipe carrier at the ceremonies. I often take tobacco to her, and we have a chance to visit. Tobacco is the most sacred symbol in the Indian tradition. My friend is an elder even though she is ten years younger than I am. Being called an elder has to do with experience, knowledge, and wisdom; it has nothing to do with age. It is a status that commands respect and is something you earn by experiencing life.

Lena Desizlets
Born: October 22, 1896

Lena Desizlets was born in the vicinity of Fosston, Minnesota. She attended government schools for several years and was married at age eighteen. She has had seven children, six of whom are living. She now lives alone in a house that has been her home for seventy-one years, in Bemidji. She states, "I'm probably more independent than I should be."

As a youngster, I was expected to work in the house. I did a lot of the usual housework things, and after I was thirteen, I did most of the cooking. In the summertime, we had a large garden. We canned all that food, and we were great about finding and picking wild fruit. As soon as things started to ripen, we would get started and would work way into the fall. We made jelly and jam from the fruit and canned the vegetables. We learned a lot of this from my dad, who was also a great deer hunter. He would remember from his fall hunting where the fruit was. All my brothers and sisters did this together. One of the older kids would stay home with the kids who were too little to go along. My dad would hitch up the team and pack a picnic lunch; almost the whole family would go. As soon as the little ones were old enough, they were given a little pail and would pick, too.

  We lived on a little farm. We raised pigs and cattle, and my dad raised only enough grain to feed them. Our farm was very wooded, so my father earned his living by cutting wood.

  When I was seven, I stayed for a while with my grandparents, who spoke only French. After I had been with them for a year, I came home and started to go to a government school in Beaulieu, Minnesota. My dad would take us down in the fall, and we would stay all winter until June, when school was out. Some French people at school would interpret for me when I couldn't understand, but I had to learn English in a hurry. Then in the summer we would go home again, and I would help out with whatever work there was to do. I went to school in Beaulieu for two years, then to Pipestone for three, and to White Earth for a year.

  Being in school was like being in the military — lots of rules. We were given our food and clothes. On Sundays we wore sort of a dark uniform so we all looked alike. We weren't allowed off the premises unless we had an escort. At night we lined up for roll call. We marched to meals. They lined us up by size, and everything started and stopped by whistle and bell. We marched everywhere.

  We went to school for half a day, and we worked for half a day. Sometimes we worked in the laundry, sorting clothes and ironing. When we worked in the kitchen, we would cook great big hunks of meat in big pans. The girls would help prepare the food, and the boys would do the gardening. The girls did only housework. The classes we took were very basic—reading, writing, and English.

When I was very young, before I went to school, we spoke mostly English at home. My mother was trying to learn English, too; when she got married, she spoke only French. No one spoke the Indian language in our home. I didn't even know that my dad could understand it or speak it. Our language was really a mix when my grandparents were around. My dad's mother was Chippewa Indian and part French. My mother's people were French, and my great-great-grandfather was from Sweden. When he arrived from Sweden, he docked in Canada and wandered down into Minnesota. He was taken in by Native Americans and lived with them until he met some people of his own culture and eventually married. He ended up down by Stillwater, where he owned acres of land and a trading post.

Speaking different languages and going to different schools, I didn't turn out to be much of a scholar. When I left Pipestone, I was only in the third or fourth grade. I returned to White Earth then for about a year. After that I just stayed home and helped out with whatever there was to do. We had a big family, and there was a lot to be done.

There was not much social life that I remember. The farmers would get together sometimes for picnics and dances. I met my future husband at a dance. He was born in New York City and was an orphan who had been adopted by a couple who lived in Afton, Minnesota. They had bought land from the Indians near Fosston, and that's how I happened to meet him. We were married when I was eighteen.

I was allotted some government land, so we moved to this land south of Fosston on the White Earth Reservation. Back then the parents would go to a government office to get the allotted 160 acres for their children. You had to take what land was available, so the children got land in different places. They could do with it what they wanted, work the land or sell it. That's why the land became a checkerboard, some of it owned by Native Americans and some by the white people, who bought it.

We had a wonderful life on this land. We had to break this ground before we could farm it. It was hard work. We shared machinery with my husband's folks. After a while, we sold this land and farmed in different places, mostly renting. We had seven children, but one died in infancy. The other six are living, all in Minnesota and North Dakota. They come home quite often, but I'd like to see them more.

In 1924 we moved to the Bemidji area, and I have lived in the same home for seventy-one years. My husband worked for two or three companies all those years. During the war, he delivered groceries to many small towns, up as far north as International Falls. I helped him for years on the truck. The company didn't hire me, but I helped anyway.

We were taught very little about our Native American culture when we were children. Sometimes we went to visit uncles and aunts on the reservation, but the area where we lived was settled mostly by whites—Scandinavians and other northern Europeans. My dad being so much Swede, he had blue eyes and was real light until he got older. I don't think my parents were embarrassed about their Indian heritage, but they probably felt it would be easier on us kids if we didn't focus on it. They raised us that way to protect us.

I remember only once that my dad took us up to Red Lake for a powwow. I recall the dances we attended with our neighbors more clearly, where we did mostly square dances and waltzes. Maybe another reason our parents didn't teach us much about our culture is because we were all too busy working. I don't remember that life was so hard, but we were busy farming and making a living.

When my children were born, we enrolled them all at White Earth. My husband supported this so that the children would have land of their own. They didn't have to live there or farm it, but they could sell it if they wanted to and then buy someplace else.

My main job all my life has been to care for children and take care of the house. My daughter remembers that I was the one who handled the discipline. My husband worked very hard and was usually gone all day. It was easier to tend children back then. I always knew where they were and whom they were with.

I tried to teach them right from wrong. I would say, "I depend on you to do the right thing." When something went wrong for any of them, we would sit down and talk it over until we understood why it happened. Usually I could discipline them with just a look. That was enough. When the children were little, my husband and I let them know who was boss, and they had to respect what we thought was right. Of course, we didn't always know what was going on, but it wasn't too bad.

We are a close family. We can count on each other if we need help. Once my first little girl came home and asked if it was wrong to be an Indian. She had been asked her nationality at school, and she told them. One of the neighbor girls said, "You shouldn't have told them. No one would know you are Indian if you didn't tell them." I told my daughter, "No, there is nothing wrong with it. There might be some people who will look down on you because you are Indian, but don't worry about them. It's what you are yourself, inside—not your nationality—that counts."

Sue Bellefeuille grew up in Mahnomen, Minnesota, in a large family—her father, mother, and twelve siblings. She has been on the front lines of reservation political events during the past few years. Her job at the casino exposed her to some of the administration problems there. Sue is presently employed as a home health aide with a company in Mahnomen, working with families and doing "whatever needs to be done." Sue believes she is grounded in reality as a result of personal experiences. She is proud of her heritage, although she has many concerns about the future of her people.

Sue Bellefeuille
Born: May 21, 1948

I knew that if your name was McArthur, everyone knew you were Indian. My dad would just laugh when we would tell him stories about kids teasing us about being Indian. He would say, "Go tell them you were here first." We kids had all different kinds of coloring. Some of us had black hair and darker skin, and some of us were lighter skinned and blue eyed. But we were all McArthurs, and we are all still living in this area, the farthest away being Duluth. My dad's grandmother was full-blooded Chippewa, and she married a man who was half Scottish and half Irish by the name of McArthur. I'm a quarter German, a quarter Indian, a quarter Scottish, and a quarter Irish. My husband says I'm pretty bullheaded from all my nationalities, especially the German blood and Indian blood.

Although I grew up during a time when the mother stayed home and took care of the house and children, I have been employed for several years. My present job has a lot of variety. For example, some of the people I work with have had knee or hip replacements. I go in several times a week and exercise their legs for them. I make sure they do their exercises. I meet with the physical therapist, and he or she shows me what to do with the patient. Today, for example, I saw "Tom," who is bedridden. Two of us usually go in together to help his wife get him up, sponge bathe him, and get him into a wheelchair. Twelve years ago, he had a stroke; he has been recuperating at home, but his wife is really getting played out. Then I went to Waubun and helped a woman get ready for a doctor appointment. She has diabetes so bad that she has lost her eyesight. This lady is someone who needs to visit, so I talk with her.

I learn from these people. They teach me about myself. I know that many of the ailments these people have are hereditary. Diabetes is very common and so is heart disease. My mother, all her brothers, and my father died of heart attacks. My father was only sixty-two.

I have been married twice. My first husband and I were married for fifteen years and lived in several places. We were living near Chicago when we bought a resort near Park Rapids, where my twelve-year-old son and I moved after the divorce. I married again after several years and settled in Mahnomen. These were confusing years for my son, and I regret that.

My religious background was also confusing. My father was a very strong Catholic. If we missed church, we were in really big trouble with him. My mother, on the other hand, had a background that included the mission boarding schools. Her memories of the nuns at the school are very negative, so she ended up just hating the church, while my father was very strong in his beliefs. Then my son's father came from a family that was very strict in the Assembly of God church, and he too felt that religion had been forced on him. Because of this background, I have raised my son very openly about religion.

In spite of these religious conflicts, we were always aware and proud of being Indian. Dad used to tell stories about his grandma being a full-blood. Dad built a home on a lake and called it Awakaan, my grandmother's Indian name. I think my folks were so busy raising kids that they really didn't have time to give us a lot of history, but we got bits and pieces of it. My father took us to powwows in the summertime. He was a real quiet man, and I was proud of him. I compare my feelings and respect for my parents and ancestors with what I see in the young people today, and it seems to me that there is more anger and resentment now about things that have happened. This replaces the appreciation and respect for our ancestors and their way of life.

I believe we need to start taking care of our old people. If we don't take care of our elders, our young will be neglected, too. We have to do more to give our young people purpose. I am sad about the kids on the reservation and the way some of them live. Many changes need to be made, and these changes will involve politics. The casino was supposed to help us improve things financially, but, in my opinion, it has created many problems, too. There is more money because it has provided jobs, but that has made it possible for us to spend more on drinking and gambling. Right now, I don't see that we are benefiting from the casino. But if the right people were in management, I think it could be a good thing; for example, a fund could be set up to benefit old people. But we must clean up the elections first, or nothing will change.

I used to work at the bingo hall. I became very involved with the people I worked with. I really enjoyed my job for a while. There were so many connections with people, and I wanted to do things that would help these people who had been good to me. But I could see things happening that I did not like. I was encouraged to go public with what I knew and what I had seen in 1991. I was very troubled by it all, so I quit my job in March 1991. This was a very hard time. I found out things about people I had trusted that really upset me. It bothers me a lot when I see people hurting other people.

That was a strange time in my life. In most ways, I enjoyed being a part of the changes I thought would be good for the reservation. On the other hand, it caused a lot of conflict among friends and even in the family. Some things were done just to get the attention of the authorities so the whole operation could be cleaned up. Then there was trouble, because some of these things were illegal. My husband was angry with me. "You're going to end up in jail someday," he would say. Neither of us really believed that.

Besides my work and my family, one of my big interests is collectibles. Some people might call it junk, but I have found a few nice old pieces at the auctions we attend on the weekends. I wouldn't dare call the things I buy antiques. But it's fun to travel around and search out treasures. At one time, I thought I might like to own a store and sell collectibles, but right now I am just a collector.

My husband and I also enjoy traveling to powwows. We don't participate; we mostly sit and watch. The annual White Earth powwow makes me feel connected to think of what went on with our people on those same grounds over 120 years ago. Powwows are a big visiting time, like a large reunion. It brings back memories of when we were kids. There is dancing, of course, and many drummers from all over the state and Canada. They hold competitions in different categories. There is a big feast on Sunday, and anyone who wants to can eat for nothing. It's nice.

Some of us who grew up in the city missed out on learning much about our traditions. The language, for instance, was rarely heard in my family. My grandma died when I was fifteen, and my older sisters can remember going places with her and hearing the language. I only remember being called "white Indians" because we were raised in town. It would have been much different if we had grown up in Ponsford, Elbow Lake, or White Earth. I'm concerned about the future of Indian people. You know, I don't think there is a person on the reservation now who is full-blooded.

I really hope some changes can be made so people can start living and going to work without being afraid that, if they speak out, they will lose their jobs. People should not have to live in fear. I had to quit my job to get away from that fear and to have the freedom to speak out. It meant some big changes for us, but it was worth it.

Anita Fineday

Born: November 12, 1954

Anita Fineday, an enrolled member of White Earth, is the tribal attorney for the Leech Lake band of Chippewa. Born and raised in Louisville, Kentucky, she moved to Minnesota in 1988. She earned a bachelor's degree in English literature at Indiana University and her law degree at the University of Colorado in Boulder. She has worked with the Native American Rights Fund in Boulder and Anishinabe Legal Services, which provides legal representation on the Leech Lake, White Earth, and Red Lake Reservations of Minnesota. She has also served as the tribal attorney for the Mille Lacs Reservation. She is married and has two daughters—one studying archeology at Harvard University and the other attending high school in Walker, Minnesota.

My mother tells me how ironic it is that I am here on Leech Lake after she went to such great pains to get me away from the reservation. She is not a traditional woman. When she was in her teens and twenties, living on the Leech Lake Reservation, she saw the alcoholism and the lack of jobs, and she wanted to get me as far away from that as she could.

But even when we were living in Louisville, Kentucky, where I was born and grew up, northern Minnesota was home. Every year as far back as I can remember, Mom would tell me, "We're going home for the summer." I think most Indian people, even when they move away, always think of the reservation as home.

I had an unusual childhood. My parents were divorced when I was one or two years old, and my mom raised me alone. She is a registered nurse who was very independent and hard working; she worked the three-to-eleven-o'clock shift when I was young. A woman whom I call my nanny ended up sort of raising me. She'd baby-sit while my mother worked, and then, since it got so late, I'd just sleep over until the next morning. Eventually, I was with my nanny from Monday through Friday, and would spend weekends with my mom. My nanny, who is eighty-nine now, came from the hills of Kentucky; she is non-Indian. I still go back to Louisville to see her every year. She's a very loving woman, and she took very good care of me.

That was pretty much our lifestyle until I was thirteen. Then Mom got a job as a nursing instructor, the first time she ever had a regular nine-to-five kind of job, and I went to live with her full-time.

I graduated from high school in 1972 and got my degree in English literature from Indiana University in 1980. By that time, I had been married, had my oldest daughter, had gone to school, and had gotten divorced. I just knew that I had to go to college. I needed an education.

I planned to get a Ph.D. in English literature and teach, to be a college professor. To this day, English literature is still my great love. I got a fellowship to the University of Michigan and began working on my master's degree and ended up meeting my second husband and becoming pregnant with my second daughter.

As I got into the master's program, I developed a more realistic view of what the job prospects were going to be. The chances of getting employment would be very slim. So I went back to school and got my certificate to teach in high school. But I discovered something important when I did my student teaching: I am not cut out to be a high school and middle-school teacher. I really did not like these kids! They were just brats.

So I started looking for a job. I saw an ad for a technical writer to write grant reports, proposals, and a newsletter for the Native American Rights Fund in Boulder, Colorado, a law firm specializing in major-impact cases in Indian law. My experience there, where I worked with Indian attorneys every day, influenced my decision to become a lawyer. I enrolled in the University of Colorado Law School, working as a law clerk at the Rights Fund while I went to school. In the back of my mind, I think I always wanted to come to Minnesota. After I graduated, I was offered a job with Anishinabe Legal Services in Cass Lake. My second husband and I packed all our belongings into our Subaru station wagon and came up here. Everything we had fit into that car! I've been here ever since.

I got to know the reservations in northern Minnesota when I was providing legal representation to Leech Lake, White Earth, and Red Lake. This experience gave me a good broad background. Then I took a job as tribal attorney for Mille Lacs. I filed the hunting-and-fishing-treaty lawsuit while I was there. For the past three years, I've been the tribal attorney for the Leech Lake Reservation. When I came here, I saw the Indian Child Welfare Act as an area of Indian law that had been very much neglected by the all-male tribal councils. To the Leech Lake Council's credit, they've permitted me to concentrate a large part of my practice in this area. I consider it my number-one priority. I really thank them for that.

The Indian Child Welfare Act was passed by the U.S. Congress in 1978, largely in response to the amazing statistics about the removal of Indian children from their homes. The number of removals and the number of kids who absolutely and virtually disappeared were truly shocking. Think of Jacob Wetterling [a non-Indian boy who was abducted near his St. Joseph home in 1989 and has never been found]. That's an experience shared by almost every person living on the reservation in the 1950s and 1960s—having their kids removed by social workers and never knowing what happened to those children. Parental rights were often terminated, and the children were adopted out—something that occurred in a consistent and organized fashion on reservations through the 1960s.

It started in the 1920s and 1930s. As a kid in the 1950s, I remember seeing Indian people still living in what would be called tarpaper shacks. They didn't have electricity and running water. They lived a very traditional lifestyle. They still had fishing camps—not really nomadic, but certainly not a white middle-class way of living. When social workers from the Bureau of Indian Affairs or the state looked at this, they saw poverty and children not being cared for properly, so they removed them. These weren't bad people doing this. I think they truly believed this was the best thing for these kids. They believed they were acting with the best kind of missionary goals: taking care of kids whom they saw as neglected or abused.

Working here on the reservation, I see the results of that policy all the time. I see many people in their fifties, raised in a non-Indian world, coming back to the reservation to try and figure out who their relatives are. People come into my office and ask me, "Can you help me find my relatives? I think their names are such-and-such." They want answers to questions like, "Who am I? Where did I come from? Who is my family?"

The number-one goal of the Indian Child Welfare Act is to protect kids. If they must be removed from their homes for some reason, we look toward placing them on the reservation with relatives—to keep them in Indian homes. The tribes have been robbed of so much—their land, their children. Without those kids, tribes and culture will cease to exist.

One of the first things Indian people ask when they meet each other is "Where are you from?" They don't answer "Minnesota"; instead, they give the name of their tribe. That's how Indian people identify themselves to one another and also, I think, to themselves. You are a Leech Lake person, or a White Earth person, or a Red Lake person. Your identification with your tribe forms the basis of your identity.

We're fighting for our survival by fighting to keep our children. They've got to have that contact with their elders, their families, their communities, and, most important, their tribe.

I think the tribes came very, very close to losing their culture completely, especially here in Minnesota and to the west. We've already lost a hell of a lot of it. Now we're digging in, down in the trenches, and fighting to keep what we have. We are not going to lose anything else and that includes our kids.

The thing that strikes me most today is the total lack of education about Indian people in America. There are an estimated two million Indian people in the United States. Our population is estimated to have been between ten and fifty million back in the 1600s, when non-Indian people first came here. You can't look at those figures without a sense of absolute destruction, almost complete annihilation.

Last summer I took my older daughter to Harvard, where she's studying archeology, and we spent some time on the East Coast. I was struck by how many streets and cities and states and natural landmarks are named after tribes, but the tribes aren't there. They no longer exist. This country has yet to deal with that. American society as a whole has chosen to ignore what it did to Indian people. We came very close to simply not existing. I would like to see *that* included in the history books.

It's very important to me to serve as a role model, to be accessible to young girls and women on the reservation today. When Indian people reach a certain level of education and expertise in their professions, we need to return to the reservation. We owe that to our tribes—to come back and to give back.

Ann LaVoy lives on South Twin Lake near Pine Hurst and is the tribal enrollment officer for the White Earth Reservation. She served on the Mahnomen School Board and has been chairwoman of the board. Ann has also been active in two programs for the elderly: the Minnesota Board on Aging and the Headwaters Board on Aging. She also has worked with the Regional Development Commission in Bemidji. While her children were in school, she became interested in educational issues. Ann believes that parents should take some responsibility for the education of their children, but that the whole community should be involved as well. Ann is the oldest of eight children and has four children of her own.

Ann LaVoy
Born: January 6, 1938

My brothers and sisters used to tell me when I baby-sat that I was "the oldest and the meanest." I don't consider myself a *gentle* person, but I admire that quality in others. There were gentle people in my large, close family, and I know many elders who are gentle and humble. I am discovering that the people who are just now finding their roots, their "Indianness," are missing those qualities, which the Indians who grew up knowing their heritage have.

My immediate family is very close. My children genuinely like each other. They have learned closeness from the community in which we lived. One year our house was hit by lightning, and the community came forward and supported us after our house burned down. It was unbelievable the way this poor community helped us get started again. Our community was very caring and generous.

Since then our community has changed drastically. When public housing is available, some people come back from the metro area to take advantage of it. This has changed things. We used to know everyone we saw at the village store. Drug use is also a big part of the change. When I was growing up, there would be an alcoholic here or there. But now whole families are involved in drugs: users, sellers, or both. Life isn't as simple as it used to be. It's painful. Many kids don't know who their dads are. I think many of our children feel abandoned.

Federal funding to build more houses or schools is not going to solve this problem. Kids with learning disabilities are living with foster parents, grandparents, or adoptive parents, and they have no idea who their real families are. This new lifestyle is compounding problems in so many different ways: people don't feel safe anymore; kids have learning problems; people are living in public housing. HUD says you must pay a certain percentage for your rent, and they also say that drugs are not allowed on the property, but nobody enforces this.

I cannot sit back and pass judgment; I can only say what happened to me. There were people in my life who had a strong influence on me: my mom and dad, Grandma Annie, Frances Keahna's mother, and my mother's dad, Grandpa Turner. Grandpa said, "Somebody from here has to go to college." He told me, "You have to make a hole in the fence so more people can get through." He knew his heritage and could speak Ojibwe fluently. But from one generation to the next, I have seen the language disappear and values change. He wanted me to help carry on the history of our heritage.

I used to spend a lot of time with my Grandma Annie in the summer. My dad said it was my job to go up and see how she was doing and help her if she needed help. Grandma and Frances, my dad's sister, would sit there and visit; the two got together almost every day. I would stand by the screen door and listen while they sat at a big round table and talked, ate, and made their baskets. In my memory, it seems that all those days were bright and sunny. Sometimes I would turn to them and tell them in Indian that they should not speak their language because then I could not understand. They thought this was funny. We had respect for each other. For example, if I had done something wrong, my grandmother didn't scold me, but in a quiet way she let me know I had done something that was unacceptable. I enjoyed being with her. Sometimes I would ask her, "What are we going to do today?" She would say that we were going "bumming." That meant we would do anything from berry picking to going to the county fair. She would put on her new beaded moccasins, which she had made that spring, pick up her little beaded bag, and away we'd go.

I can remember Grandpa Turner saying, "An Indian is as good as his word." If you're a good Indian, your word is good. You could shake hands and tell somebody, "I'll be here with your five dollars tomorrow at noon," and you were there. There are some people left with that sense of integrity, but in general, I think it is gone. I heard someone say years ago, "Self-government without self-control is self-destruction." I still have those words on my wall at work.

I think our younger generation needs something. They are grasping. They need a place to belong, an identity. They are searching for their heritage and, in many cases, are coming up with some mixed ideas. I remember when the drums and the dancing meant much more than the kind of costume you were wearing. A lot of our young people, some of them in their thirties, are searching for that feeling. I was fortunate enough to have been raised in a way of thinking that included respect and reverence for tradition.

I grew up seeing my grandparents treated with respect. Now I see a lot of people being ignored or put down in many little ways. Once I saw a woman in a store who had to reach over the counter to pick up her change because the clerk would not put it in her hand. Sometimes I wonder how much longer we can go on living with this kind of hurt. I wonder if that's one reason we have so much alcoholism, drugs, and suicide.

I have learned so much in my job as enrollment officer. White Earth is just one of the six member reservations of the Minnesota Chippewa Tribe. The constitution article that deals with membership was established in the early 1960s, when there was a reorganization. My job is working with tribal enrollments. I've been doing it a long time. It's very precise. Just when you think you've heard it all, a new question is raised. It is confusing to most people. For example, it is conceivable that someone could have a quarter-blood quantum and not have a parent who is enrolled in any reservation in Minncsota; he or she would be denied membership because of the "parent not on the '41' roll" restriction. Does this make sense?

Applications have increased because people think money is involved. All these stories are out there about Indians getting a thousand dollars a month from the government. It is not true in this area. The process we go through is to review the application, fill out a small card for the file and a large card that shows parents' names, their degrees, when they were enrolled, where they were born, and their dates of birth. Then we send a letter of notification saying whether they were accepted or denied. We have processed 3,518 applications since 1986.

I really enjoy my work. I like to talk to people, and it feels good that they believe in me and trust me. Some of the most enjoyable interviews I've had have been with people who have been adopted. In the 1950s and early 1960s, Social Services could just walk in and take kids away with no notice or anything; the families didn't know what happened to those kids. Many of those people who knew they were Indian are now becoming tribal members through application. Most of them need assistance from the adoption services in their states to process and access records. Some of them are the neatest people I've ever talked with.

As far as education is concerned, I think some of our people stay in the system because they hope that someday they will have more say in what happens in their lives. I think our educational system should aim more at the very young, like upgrading the Head Start program. We have a good school system here and are always working to improve it. We graduated fifty-five kids the end of May, and twenty-two of those kids were Indian.

Some of our large dropout rate is due to the families that move back and forth from the metro area. Sometimes when the kids enroll, it is impossible to tell what grade they are in. We're in a society now where it's not just a family that's responsible for kids, it's the whole community, but when families move a lot, this doesn't work.

I've enjoyed being involved with the schools that my children attended. I think women make good board members because they've run families. We are the prime movers. We get the job done. At White Earth I think we have a way to go at recognizing the talents of our people, all people, and women especially.

One thing I believe in strongly is the teaching of *respect*. One day I confronted the priest who was teaching a class I was taking about his use of the word *tolerance*. I told him that tolerance was just one step above prejudice. I said, "Some of us have to learn tolerance by living it. I know who *tolerates* me, and I know who *respects* me. When you live with it all the time, you know the difference. I think we need to work on respect and integrity and get past the tolerance level." But for now, I'll take tolerance over prejudice.

Anne M. Dunn
Born: November 9, 1940

Anne Dunn, an enrolled member of the White Earth Nation, lives in Cass Lake, Minnesota. She was born at Red Lake into a family that loved telling stories and reading. She has attended many different schools and has pursued careers in nursing and education. Anne's life experiences have earned her a distinguished reputation as a storyteller and writer. Although this work keeps her very busy, she finds time to volunteer support services for recovering alcoholics, battered women, and prison inmates. Besides continuinuing this work, she seeks more time for serious writing.

This White Earthling was born at Red Lake, enrolled at White Earth, and lived for many years at Leech Lake. I spent my childhood at Red Lake and White Earth and in Minneapolis. My father was a logger and had to move around quite a bit. He was also alcoholic and could be quite abusive when he was drinking. My mother eventually had to leave him and move to Minneapolis. We lived with my grandparents in a house on Franklin Avenue that I have referred to in my newspaper columns; this house has become quite famous, even though it is no longer there. The happy part of my childhood was spent there with my grandparents. Even now, when I drive by, I can almost see Grandpa sitting on the front porch of that house.

 We lived in many houses in Minneapolis, so I went to a lot of different schools. I'm not sure why we moved so much, but I suspect it may have been because we couldn't pay the rent. It was so hard trying to find a place in a social group when we moved so much. I finally gave up on having friends. Learning to read and then reading were my great liberators. I didn't read junk. My grandmother would read to me: Stevenson, Kipling, Alcott, Whittier. Some of these authors were heroes to my grandmother, and I had a hero of my own, Henry David Thoreau. She didn't explain much when she read to me. I just had to pick it up as she read. I think it was good for me. My grandmother and I admired very idealistic people, like Mahatma Gandhi. She spoke of Gandhi with such deep respect and admiration that, as a child, I thought they were close personal friends. We were devastated when he was assassinated.

 I graduated from Cass Lake High School in 1959, but I must say I never really enjoyed school. What I loved was building tree houses or digging holes in the ground. In school I didn't feel like I was very clever. I didn't like feeling dumb, so school was unpleasant. Many years later, I met one of my teacher's professional friends in a library. She said, "Ruth always said that you would go far. She said someday that you would write a book." I thought, "My God, she believed in me! She should have told me!" The periods of actual success during my childhood were very small and far apart.

 My grandfather had been a carpenter, and I admired that work. I thought

I would like to carry a big black lunch box and go to work to build things. I took a test and found out that I did have the aptitude to be a carpenter, but instead I went to Albuquerque to the Indian School of Practical Nursing. It seemed more *practical*. This was an incredible experience, not because I was studying to become an LPN but because of the women I met there. And they were all like me: they thought they didn't know anything either. We were discovering our potential.

When I graduated, I got a letter from Hubert H. Humphrey congratulating me for finishing in the top six out of forty students. That doesn't seem like very much, but to me it was a major accomplishment because I thought I was dumb. So there I was, even tutoring some of the other students. In New Mexico I was smart; in Minnesota I was dumb. I figured it must have been the sunshine!

Before I went to Albuquerque, I had worked summers as a nanny and as a carhop at White Castle. My mother did not discourage me from trying new things. She was a terrific mother. I wish everybody had a mother like mine. My grandmother, my mother, and the Albuquerque girls were all important women in my life. I have good memories of them. I recently gave my daughter Esther a photograph of all of us at a picnic in Arizona. I can still remember clearly how we looked in that picture.

I have been married twice. The first relationship produced six children—three girls and three boys—all beautiful and talented, but some of them don't know it yet. I also have about a dozen grandchildren. Most of them live quite close to me so I see them a fair amount. They all have lives of their own, and I think sometimes that I might be a bit boring for them. We all have different interests. My second marriage is to a man who is very proud to be a full-blooded Anishinabe Ojibwe. He's enrolled at Leech Lake. We have a really terrific relationship, and I think if anything ever happened to him, I would just have to go on alone because there is just nobody like him.

I got into storytelling as soon as I learned how to talk. I would tell stories, and my father would sit on the floor and listen. My mother was also a storyteller. Both my parents could make a story out of anything. Natural-born storytellers. I found I had a good memory for the stories I liked. Now I have a collection in my head. I like to tell women stories and stories with children in them and about how young people do heroic things for the welfare of the whole community. Those are my heroes. I remember being told that there was a time when the storytellers would start a story with the first snowfall and tell that story all winter long into the spring. I think what has been passed down are pieces of those long winter stories.

A lot of time was spent inside in the winter. People would gather in the evenings to hear long stories told by a highly respected epic storyteller. This would go on for many nights, everyone coming back the next night to hear the next part. What else was there to do? We heard stories about our relatives and heroes who went to the other side a long time ago. Although we never got to meet them, we feel we know our ancestors from these stories and have very personal feelings for them. This close connection with our ancestors is why we engage in political struggle today. We remember our grandmothers and our great-grandfathers and all they went through and how they did not quit. I feel I was born into this human struggle, and I accept it. It has helped to create me and make me who I am. Sometimes I even rejoice in it.

My father was a magnificent storyteller, but he was also an alcoholic and abusive at times. I saw a lot of abuse as a child; I saw a lot of drinking. When we moved to Minneapolis, there were more people in my life who were drinking. They were very nice to children, but I have seen people beaten bloody right in front of me. Alcohol was all around. I grew to hate alcohol, the whole alcoholic experience, and I still do. When the people who did these things are told what they did, they can't remember it, and they call it fun. They laugh and say, "Gee, did I do that?" I wonder when they had all the fun, because when I saw them, they were lying in their own blood or were puking and sick. Some people may have been enamored by it, but for me it was definitely not the way to go. I've never been engaged in drinking. I don't do alcohol; I don't do drugs.

My grandparents never drank at all, and they weren't abusive to each other; when I was with them, I was rescued. It was heaven. I'd come to heaven on

Franklin Avenue in Minneapolis. It was so nurturing to be with them. My grandmother encouraged fantasy. Maybe that's why I have become a storyteller. We rely on mystery and magic. Children enjoy it. I do, too. I don't think I will ever have enough gray hair that would somehow make a medicine in my brain that would forbid me from enjoying magic and mystery.

I don't think that my spiritual journey is separate. I think it's all woven together like a beautiful braid, and it's all part of my life. Looking back on this journey, I can see how significant certain people were, but I think reading was what taught me the most. I read anything I could get my hands on. I used to take a book and an apple and maybe a cheese sandwich and go out early in the morning. I'd run out in the woods somewhere, sit down, and read my book and eat my apple and my sandwich. Later in the day, I'd look up and say, "Well, look at that; it's dark. I'd better go home." I don't know if anyone worried about me. No one said they did.

I believe everyone has a dream, but sometimes we avoid it by living out someone else's dream. I don't want to be rich, but I do want to live out my own dream and make my living at it. And that's what I'm doing with my storytelling.

I've been told that when we get to the end of our road, we will be asked three questions: "Did you enjoy your journey?" and "Were you kind to your relatives?" The third question is a secret because it's just for you. It will be a surprise. Whoever is asking it will probably know the answer, but it will be asked anyway so that you can sort it out yourself. Tantalizing, isn't it?

Bonnie Faye Wadena
Born: August 12, 1942

Bonnie Wadena was born, raised, and educated in the villages of Nay-tah-waush and Mahnomen. As a youngster, she also lived in Crookston, Minnesota. She is one of thirteen children, eight girls and five boys. Since Bonnie's husband has been imprisoned, she has welcomed her family's support. "They just stop in," she says. "They want to know if I need anything. I really appreciate that." Her loyalty to her family is very strong. Both her parents and grandparents raised Bonnie. She married Chip Wadena when she was twenty, and they lived in the Crookston area for about five years, while Chip worked in the beet plant. They had six children and also were foster parents to several Native American children for fifteen years. Bonnie feels betrayed by the opinions expressed in the media about her husband and his problems with the law. She believes that promises and trust have been broken.

My memories of my early schooling in Crookston are not pleasant. I remember kids running around teasing us by patting their mouths and going "la-la-la-la." Maybe it happened only once, but I remember not wanting to go to school after that. I recall one day when my sister Leah had been teased; we were standing on the playground, crying. I never wanted to go back and transferred to the school in Nay-tah-wausch. But my sister stayed and eventually got along okay.

My grandfather Harold Emerson served on a tribal council and a school board. Daddy always worked; we were never hungry. My memories of childhood are more or less happy. We didn't have much, but we really didn't want for anything either. I don't remember any periods of sadness, drinking, fighting, or anything like that. I sort of knew that Mom was the boss, but I don't recall any major disagreement about this. Although my father was not an Indian, we did attend powwows and ceremonies. I don't recall really learning very much about my heritage as a child. I wish I had paid more attention.

My grandfather on my mother's side (the Emersons) was full-blooded Indian. I've wondered if there are any full-blooded Indians anymore—not any that I know. I have a suspicion that my mother and her generation turned against the Indian heritage during the years of the mission schools. I know they quit using the language and were discouraged from practicing any Native American traditions.

As far as religious practices are concerned, all of us were raised Catholic, but I like to attend church with my daughter and her husband. I love the music and the fellowship I find there. I wish I knew more about the history of our religious beliefs and particularly about medicine men. My impression as a child was that medicine men were just like doctors. I know it was a long process to become a medicine man and be able to help people. Both Chip and I can remember times when our mothers were very sick and were healed by medicine men. Religion has always played a big part in my life, and I have needed that faith to get through some of the things that have happened lately.

Since Chip has been in prison, I find that I get angry easily. I need prayer and I need my children, who have faith, to help me see things in a positive way. My kids remind me to pray for those who have caused bad things to happen to our family. Now that Chip is away from home, my mood can change from hour to hour. I have to keep busy and talk with my kids regularly to keep my mood up.

Right now I am working as an aide at Nay-tah-waush School. I need the money, and I don't like to ask my kids for help. Sometimes I can't go to visit Chip because I don't even have gas money. So I get mad at that. I get mad if I have a flat tire. It reminds me of the material things that are really not important to me, but that I need to get by. My children too are hurt quite often because they hear things from other people that are not true. The kids get impatient and discouraged. It is very hard not knowing how long Chip will be gone and how things will turn out in the courts; sometimes we all feel hopeless. That's when we need my son-in-law to say that everything is going to be all right.

Most of my life, I have been a homemaker and a mother. But I did work for a while as a cook for Elderly Nutrition and then as an aide in the classroom for Head Start. When I got certified, I was a Head Start teacher for about five years. I quit a few years ago, when I began to have a hard time being with three- and four-year-olds all day; it didn't seem fair for me or the kids to stay on. Now I'm trying to get hired at the new clinic at White Earth, but I think my name, Wadena, may hurt my chances of being hired. This is a very tough situation.

What has happened to Chip and our family is very confusing to all of us. When the indictments came down, Chip couldn't tell us anything, couldn't explain what was happening. And the court process is very long, and much of it I don't understand. But from the stories I've heard, I feel Chip didn't have a chance to explain. I try to protect Chip by not telling him how hard things are at home. It does no good for him to know, because he can't do anything about it from prison. For example, my kids and I tried to keep the store going, but we were working for nothing just to make the payments; we finally had to close and get paying jobs.

Not knowing what is going to happen or how long Chip will be gone is also very hard. His sentence was fifty-one months, but it has been appealed. When it's all over and Chip is back home, I would like to move away from here.

I hope Chip won't have anything more to do with Indian politics. I want to get away, but I want to be close enough so we can still see our kids.

I am very grateful for the support I've received from my family and from friends. There is a woman up the road who is like my sister. She has done so much to help me get through this. I honestly don't know how people can make it through this kind of tragedy without the support of family and friends.

All I can really say about this tragedy is that my perspective on the whole story is totally different from that of many people who base their ideas on what they read in the papers. I know that Chip was on the reservation for twenty years, and during that time the number of employees went from seventeen to about two thousand. Chip was responsible for a lot of good things happening for people. I firmly believe that he did nothing wrong. When you start looking into the details of any business, it can get very complicated, but the whole story needs to be printed. And I know that the whole, true story has not yet been told.

In the meantime, I will try to keep my life together and wait and watch and try to keep the faith with the help of my family.

Marcie Rendon lives in Minneapolis with her three teenage daughters. She has a degree in social work and Native American studies from Moorhead State University and a master's degree in early child development. She has worked in the field of social services in many capacities, but her main interests are writing and art. She is currently working on a project called "I Am More Than Just a Postcard" that involves visual art, video, and photography. Marcie strongly believes that mental health depends on people reaching out and supporting each other. She enjoys her freelance writing assignments and hopes to someday combine all her experiences into a "real book," a best-seller that will pay her bills.

Marcie Rendon
Born: March 2, 1952

I arrived in the Phillips neighborhood of Minneapolis in 1978, pregnant and with a two-year-old daughter. Phillips was like a reservation in the city, where all the Indian people lived. This is where one would find the Indian Center, the Little Earth Housing Project, and all the Indian bars. In the past seven years, the neighborhood has changed. It now has the highest percentage of people of color of any neighborhood in the metro area. The statistics of Phillips match any Third World country in terms of poverty, crime, and disease. When you just drive through the area, it appears to be a working-class neighborhood, with single-family homes and grass and fences; it really doesn't look like the ghetto that it is.

When I first arrived, I made a decision not to drink. I knew I needed a job and a strong support system. I found a sober community of Native people and attended AA meetings at the Indian Center. The Indian Health Board also had a building where there were meetings; we had get-togethers, potlucks, Christmas parties, and socials. These activities made it much easier to be there.

For several years, I worked in a prison program, helping prepare the inmates to take a GED [graduate equivalency degree] test and to learn coping skills to use when they got out. Then I worked for a youth-counseling agency with adolescent sex offenders for five years. I worked in this area until 1991, when I became really physically sick. While I was ill, I went back through my journals, which I've been writing ever since I can remember. I noticed that I wrote on nearly every page that what I really wanted to do was raise my girls, sew, and write. I decided then that I would seriously pursue writing. I didn't know what this meant, but I decided to try to make a living for my daughters and me with my writing.

Since 1991 I've done anything connected with writing that would pay. I've written everything from poetry to a small book on entrepreneurship for Native Americans that was used in schools for a Junior Achievement Program. A lot of my poetry has been published in magazines, newspapers, and anthologies, and I've been working on a book called *The Powell Summer.* For about a year, I wrote for *The Circle,* a newspaper that comes out of the Native American community, and I even tried my hand at writing a radio play. This led to more play writing, and I received some awards through the Playwrights Center. A portion of one of my plays was read and performed at the Southern Theatre here in the Cities.

Looking back on how I got into writing as a career, I can see that language has always been my biggest interest. I knew how to read and write when I started kindergarten. I recall that my first three years of school were mostly spent sitting in the back of the room writing little stories. They didn't know what to do with a kid who already knew how to read and write. Writing kept me sane during my school years. The social-service part of my career happened because of the idea that Native American women are supposed to give back to the community. I was good at social work and I enjoyed it, but all the while I really wanted to write, create, and make things.

I started seeing that the creative things I loved could bring hope to people. I believe I am better at helping people this way than working in systems and being boxed in by bureaucracies. I always felt squashed. Now, with the creative stuff I am doing, it feels like everything just keeps getting bigger and bigger, and it is true and right for me.

Our social life is centered on the Native Arts Circle and my family and long-time friends. These are the people with whom we spend Christmas, attend powwows, and celebrate birthdays. All these people are my family.

My three girls are incredibly talented, beautiful, and brilliant. Those three things all make teenage years harder. And raising girls in the inner city is insane! That is why we have been talking about moving out of the city. My two older girls studied media at the Minnesota Arts High School. They have both worked for the Phillips community television program, doing community programming. One of the programs was about violence in the home. The girls and I like to sit around, talk, eat, and laugh together. Sometimes we attend powwows. The youngest girl has a jingle dress, and the oldest does fancy dances.

Living in the Native American community does more to instill the values than saying anything. My girls have observed at powwows and ceremonies that Native American people treat each other differently from the larger society. It has been easy to build our extended family of nonblood relatives because the boundaries aren't rigid here. But my daughters are teenagers and have tried most things that other teens try. They have to break barriers and try things on their own. It was scary sometimes, and I worried and screamed a lot, ranted and raved. But they are home now and in school. Sometimes the girls notice that we are the only Indians in the place, and they will mention it. But I believe we belong everywhere; this is ours. My daughters get this message by watching me, and they know they are free to be and go where they choose. They don't feel the shyness I used to feel. They do things I never would have dreamed of doing.

The spiritual base I grew up with was not one of any particular denomination. I am a woman, I am a mother, I am a part of a family, and I believe in the connectedness of everything: the physical body, the continuation of generations, and the spiritual connection. One of my earliest memories about religion was the time a group of white kids came out from town. We were sitting on this big log over the river, and they said I was going to hell because I wasn't baptized. First, I didn't know what "hell" was. Second, I didn't know what "baptized" was. And I was absolutely convinced that nobody could hate me enough to send me to hell once they explained to me what it was. I just had this concept of myself as "good." If this God that they were talking about is really a loving God, then there was no way he could hate me enough to do something bad to me. That's my earliest memory of religion. I still don't believe in hell or in Christianity. It's not something I have taught my girls. I believe that everything is holy and that all people are just people.

My spirituality has kept me alive and sane. I have never felt alone spiritually, and this feeling didn't come from how I was raised or from Christianity. The only way I can explain it is that during the worst times in my life, something sustained me, something from the other side, the other world.

The thing I wonder most about is oppression. There was a push to exterminate us as a people. It didn't work, but we have become invisible. It's like we don't exist. The image of our people is stuck somewhere in the past two centuries. Systemized oppression has been internalized. We don't need an outside oppressor anymore, like the churches or government agencies. We do it to ourselves. We need conversations now about how to recover. How do we recover from planned extinction?

We are the survivors of a war, and we carry the same psychological scars as any people who have survived armed conflict and witnessed war. Now we need to regain our own power from within and stop attacking our own leaders. We need to quit this internalized "divide and conquer" thinking.

Part of the problem is that tribal governments are modeled after a white man's system—a system that, in my mind, is like a rotten apple. I think it is a waste of time to put energy into something that is decaying. We need to build and create new thinking based on the best of our history. There is something good about building from the inside out, building family and community based on strengths that already exist. The result is much stronger than tribal politics or the United States government.

You look at nature and see that anything that grows and is healthy has been nurtured. If people spent more time nurturing, caring, and loving, many things would flourish, and there would not be so much decay. A garden grows better when there is good soil, plenty of rain, lots of sun, and when the moon comes out when it is supposed to. That life has to be a struggle is just one of the lies we've been told.

It's pretty amazing to me that I have survived. I look at my daughters and realize that I have been with them nearly every day of their lives. In that sense, for my girls and me, I've broken the cycle of the disruption of families that began with the war, the boarding schools, the foster homes, and the chemical addiction. I'm here with them and I'm alive. We're helping each other recover, and it's really good.

No one can give power to another person. It is something each person has as a birthright. The project I'm presently working on is about being locked in the past. We are more than the pictures you see on a postcard. Today we are people with our own power and our own futures.

Delores Rousu

Born: August 26, 1947

Delores Rousu was raised in the White Earth area by her grandparents. She was the fourth of nine children. Delores was fifteen years old and living with her mother and stepfather when her mother died in a truck accident. Truancy problems resulted in her placement in a residential center; after that she lived for while with a doctor's family in Minneapolis and then, for three years, in a foster home. She married a man from Detroit Lakes, Minnesota, who came from a family of fifteen children. Delores has six children and lives with her husband, David, near Calloway, Minnesota, where they support themselves in traditional ways: cutting wood, harvesting maple syrup, and leeching.

I don't remember growing up anywhere except with my grandma and grandpa. They took care of me and took me to powwows and taught me about who I was. I knew who my mother was, but I never really lived with her until I was about fifteen, so I didn't really know her. My grandma was "Mom" and my grandpa was "Grandpa." They were my family. My grandmother was the disciplinarian. She was the one who set down the rules. This was my home.

I'm still in touch with my brothers and sisters, but there wasn't a whole lot of togetherness when we were growing up. My memory is that we were all sort of mixed up and mingled with each other as friends, not as brothers and sisters.

I was a rabble-rouser and got into trouble here and there. I did my share. The probation officer who was assigned to me for my truancy problems turned out to be one of my best friends. This was a good relationship. But my life continued down the path of truancy, and I ended up in custodial care. This wasn't all bad either, because there is some security in being locked up. Later I was placed with a family that was kind of like a "work home," and that also turned out to be good for me. It was a family of four: a doctor, who was Japanese, and his wife and children. They protected me from some of the things that could have hurt me. But I left at age fifteen and went back with my mother. Some of my old friends followed me there.

I have found that a lot of women my age have struggled with some of the same issues I do. I believe this is true because as children we were taught to "see nothing, hear nothing, speak nothing." When people are afraid to talk, a lot of corruption takes place inside. Silence makes us sick.

If I could turn back the pages, I would like to go back to the time when my mother was living and say, "I'm sorry about hurting you." But you can't go back. Those times are gone. Then I look to the future and wonder what I would have done without grandparents and what the kids today would do without grandparents. Many young people are kind of lost; there is not much guidance for them because there is so much alcohol abuse around here. These kids feel left out, like no one cares for them. I don't believe things will change for these kids until they have somebody in their lives who cares for them.

My life has been filled with people outside of my family who have cared for me. I was grateful for this, but I also remember always looking for a purpose for my life, wondering where I was going. My second foster home (where both my sister and I lived for a while) was significant in my life. If I had to pick a father in my life, it would be the husband there. He was nice to me and included me in a lot of activities. My foster mother appeared to be jealous, and that created a problem for my relationship with her. Then my sister, who was a lot darker skinned than I, left because she said she didn't want to be raised by a bunch of white people, including me.

When people ask me about my confusion in finding a place to feel comfortable with my own heritage and white society, I would reply that we are all people, all human, created by the same maker. Living with the Kim family, who were Asian American, I found out that skin color doesn't matter. We got along great. I think the important things are inside each individual and determine how each of us looks at life.

My children range in age from seventeen to thirty. My youngest is still living with me. The next oldest is working at the casino as a blackjack dealer. I hate that place; I wish it would blow up. It has wrecked too many families. It has provided jobs, but it has done harmful things to the people on the reservation.

My youngest is the only one at home, and I have been very involved with the completion of his education. I took him out of school when he was in the tenth grade because I didn't like what I could see happening to his attitude. Besides, he had always been an A or B student, but in the tenth grade, it seemed that nobody cared anymore if he made it or not. I said to him, "Joe, you're not a follower, you're a leader. And you must put into practice the gifts that God gave you."

My son more or less stayed at home, worked on his lessons, and received his credits. I would take him up to the Alternative Learning Center every two weeks, and he would test out and go on. When he returned to school, they asked him, "What are you doing here?" He said that he hadn't quit school; he had continued and he was back to finish. Another one of my sons and his wife have worked recently in the Alternative Learning Center. They both care a great deal about their students reaching their potential.

One reason that we chose this alternative education was because I wasn't happy with the communications I was having with his teachers. I wanted firsthand information about his progress, but I was not getting it. The school said it was not a "baby-sitting service." I believe this was what they thought I wanted. But I just wanted my son to learn. I saw more potential in him, and I didn't understand why he wasn't performing better. He was capable; he just wasn't doing it.

After all this, after raising six kids, I've decided that what I must do is "let go and let God." I want to say to my kids, "Get up. Grow up. Get out of here. Go make your own life." It hasn't been easy.

I often wonder where all my religious beliefs came from. I think I was a Christian person who accepted the Lord when I was about twelve years old. I have felt many, many times that I am not worthy of God's love and that I got seriously into religion too late for my kids' sake. I remember hearing, "Bring a child up in the way of the Lord. When they get older, they'll wander, but they will come back." I'm hanging on to that thought.

My children, like me, have had questions about who they really are. There are people now who are coming back and saying, "We're Indian; we were born and raised here, and we want our old traditions back." I'm saying, "It's in the past. Let it be. Keep what we know for sure, and let the rest be."

My individual feeling is that no one will really find what he or she wants until they find their God.

God helps me through a lot of things. One day in circle at our church, I said, "For the longest time, I put corner shelves in my house. When things were going good, I would say, 'Okay, God, you can sit on the shelf for now. I don't need you right now.' But then the deep valleys would come, and I would say, 'I can't get up. Come help me now. Get down off that shelf. I need you now.' Finally, I just went around the house and tore every corner shelf down and said, 'You can't sit on the shelf. I've got to have you with me every minute because life is a struggle.'" And that's me.

I don't sit and read the Bible every day. But I pray every day that I will have the time to do that someday. Right now I just go where I am led.

My life now is very involved with the traditional pursuits of my husband, David. Until I met him, I had never been in a canoe, had no idea what maple sapping was or what it meant to harvest wild rice. I didn't even know what a spear of wild rice looked like when I married David and he said, "Hey, let's go ricing." And we went ricing.

I go with him sometimes on the job, but mostly I'm the one who does the selling and marketing. I just take things one day at a time and do what has to be done. I don't try to see into the future.

As far as current events are concerned, politics and the like, I just try to ignore it. It gets to be too much to understand, all the different factions. They talk about making changes, but it always comes down to the same old thing. Over and over again, we face the same issues. Nothing changes. Then I remember what I learned as a child: you're better off if you see nothing, hear nothing, speak nothing. I guess that's what I am doing.

My Indian heritage and its lore have been brought to me by my mother-in-law and my husband. As a child, I went to powwows with my grandparents and was very impressed with them. I danced when I was a kid. I never had any regalia or anything, but I danced anyway. It was impressive, and I will never forget it. But Christianity is the real spiritual force in my life, and that is what guides me now.

Irene Auginaush-Turney was born and raised in Rice Lake, Minnesota, and lives there still. Her three brothers and two sisters live nearby. She currently sits on the White Earth Tribal Council as a district representative. Irene has worked to educate her community members about their right to have a voice and a right to vote. Her main love, however, is teaching children about their heritage and teaching parents how to convey an appreciation for this heritage to their children.

Irene Auginaush-Turney
Born: June 26, 1952

I believe my father would have liked his first-born to have been a son. But I spent a lot of time with my dad. I remember cutting firewood with him. He was a "smoke chaser" for the DNR [Department of Natural Resources]; he sat in a tower in the highland hills up here. I used to climb that tower with him and sit in that little room and watch for smoke. We would eat our lunch up there and take naps. Now I wonder how I ever dared to do it; at the top of the ladder was a little trapdoor I had to climb through to get to the room. But I did it, and I learned about the gauge he used to judge distance, and I watched and listened to him as he radioed reports to headquarters. Back on the ground, I danced with my father at the powwows from the time I was two years old. These are wonderful memories.

When my mom and dad went to pick potatoes, sometimes we kids went with them. I can remember having picnics in the woods with them. If they were working where we couldn't go along, we stayed with my grandparents. I gained a lot of my strength and much of my knowledge of traditions from my grandparents.

Someone asked me once during one of the parenting classes I was teaching, "What was the greatest sense of pride you had, or how did you know that your mom and dad loved you?" I replied that they called me "our girl"; they would say something to me and address me as "my girl." I felt their love and approval immediately.

After I had my children, I decided that I probably was not one of the "homemaker" types, baking bread and everything. So I started as a volunteer for the Head Start program. Then I became a bus aide, a classroom aide, a bus driver, an assistant teacher, and finally a teacher.

One of the things I'm proud of is that I brought my uncle from Red Lake with his drum into the classroom to teach my students how to dance. Then I thought we might as well have a feast; we'll feed the parents who come to watch the children dance. We're coming up on our twelfth annual Head Start powwow this year. We feed about five hundred people every year, all with volunteer help.

Dancing is one of the traditions that gives me a feeling that's hard to explain. It is like coming out of church, a cleansing and refreshing feeling that makes me happy. I wanted to pass this on to the kids. Now several kids dance who did not before. All my own children danced at one time, and one of them still does.

My background probably explains my interest in the cultural traditions and why I think it's so important for teachers and day-care providers to have this knowledge. I am on the State Advisory Board for Cultural Dynamics. A state law was passed in 1990 that early-childhood educators must have training in cultural dynamics. The committee developed the curriculum, and I became one of the trainers. I believe in this work so strongly because it is such a big part of a person's self-esteem. I think all of us need to value our heritage and culture in order to feel good about ourselves. Kids don't raise their hands and ask questions if they lack confidence or feel any shame. One of the worst things I saw in a Head Start classroom was a three- or four-year-old walking with his head down, acting ashamed.

I was appointed to the district representative position when the tribal leadership changed hands. My background as a teacher and a parent trainer and my experience doing contract work for a year for Head Start and in Indian child welfare and foster care qualified me for the position. I am an advocate for the people, so I didn't hesitate to respond. Although I was appointed at first, I have since run in four elections in two years, and I've now held the office for two years.

The reality of this job and the politics involved have sometimes been very painful. It is one of the biggest challenges I have had in my life. I have lost some friends, and others have tried to be my friend because of my position. Politics really does crazy things, even among family members. With some of the decisions I have to make, no matter which way I vote, someone is going to oppose it. When we came into office, it was decided that we were going to have an open and fair government. It's time that people trust their own voices, realize they have a right to an opinion. And it's time they become involved in their government. Sometimes I have been appalled by how Native Americans treat one another. During times of crisis, I can go for three or four days with very little sleep, but then comes a time when I ask myself why I am beating my head against the wall.

In a nutshell, I guess I do it because I believe I know how most Native Americans feel. I've lived the life that many of them live. I've lived on welfare; I've been a single parent; I've lived off the land. I know what it's like to go out and look for a job when very few people out there want to hire you. I know how hard it is to be in school and be made fun of. I know all the racist things that I went through in school. I think I can speak for the people, and I want to make a difference.

When I really get discouraged, I find my strength in many traditional ways: praying, putting out tobacco, talking to my husband, and being listened to. I talk to a higher power for guidance and strength. I was raised in the Episcopal church, and I'm also an Ojibwe hymnal singer. We sing at wakes and funerals, and we have Ojibwe hymn sings. I have done this for as long as I can remember.

I regret that I never learned the language. My father speaks fluently, but I don't understand it. My parents and grandparents all went to Indian boarding schools, where they were discouraged, even punished, if they used the language. My grandmother tells stories about running away from the schools when things got too hard. As a child, I thought these stories were very exciting, and I would ask her to tell them over and over again.

I was given an Indian name—Bagamwewedamokwe—by friends of my grandparents when I was a child. I've shortened it to "Thunder Is Coming," but my dad says it means that sound you hear when thunder is way off in the distance, and all of a sudden it's upon you, rain and thunder right above you.

As for my future, I really don't plan on making politics my life career. I would like to get back to my work in cultural dynamics and parent training. I want to mend that circle of passing on traditions that we seem to have lost. The circle was broken when children were taken away from their parents and raised in schools. Many of them learned harsh discipline there, and that has become a part of their parenting in this generation. I believe you parent the way you were parented. The only way I can see this break can be mended is to go out and teach. In my teaching, I have found out that recalling good childhood memories can be very effective. Almost all the good memories that the group members come up with have to do with things they did as families—sliding in the snow, going fishing, going on picnics or to the fair. We look at bad memories, too, and almost all of those involve drinking. I tell the parents to decide what kinds of memories they want to give their children.

Joan Staples

Born: August 23, 1942

Joan Staples is an enrolled member of the White Earth Reservation who now lives in Tacoma, Washington, with her two children. Her experiences have encouraged her to embrace her heritage and to recognize her role as a woman in contemporary society. In 1991 she was instrumental in opening a center for urban Indians that offers classes in the Indian language, traditions, and culture, as well as providing other general assistance. Joan has a degree in psychology from Seattle Pacific University.

The Bemidji area was home for my mother and father and their ten children. My childhood memories are a mix of carefree days and incidents of prejudice. My parents didn't explain our heritage, being half-Indian and half-Finnish. With ten children, they probably were too busy. The extent of our native awareness was visiting our grandfather in Cass Lake; he would give us maple-sugar candy at Christmas. I don't recall many positive things about being Indian, but I do remember hearing derogatory comments about Indians coming to town to spend their per capita allowances.

My school counselor told me I was not college material and that I should consider a tech school. I knew that many Indians who stayed in northern Minnesota ended up going to Minneapolis—to the Indian ghetto, as they called it. I didn't want that for myself, so I took a bus to Seattle to baby-sit my sister's children. There I could pretend I wasn't Indian. I cut my hair, dressed real fancy, and got an office job. I denied who I was. I had the job, clothes, and friends, but I was miserable inside.

Eventually I married and had a child. Now I had done everything the dominant culture said I needed to do to be happy. I had a husband, a child, a home, two cars, and money for material goods and travel. We spent a few years like this and were really into the drinking scene. But I decided I couldn't spend my life like that; it was not the way I wanted to live. I needed more education.

My husband was threatened by my return to school at age thirty-three. It was hard getting started, but once I got through the first quarter with a 4.0 grade average, I loved it. I started learning about Indians, and something started stirring in me. I took lots of classes and participated in local reservation events. My non-Indian husband did not understand why I was doing this, there was a lot of conflict, and we ended up divorcing.

After I graduated with a degree in psychology, my daughter and I moved near the Colville Indian Reservation. I fell in love with it. I worked at the church, at the newspaper, and in the school, teaching kids about their heritage. I wrote a grant that brought in community people to teach about traditional ways and about being a Colville. When I worked on the newspaper, I really tried to focus on positive information about what was happening in Indian country. I stayed there almost eight years and married again and had a son.

During this time, I was shocked to learn that Indians can be prejudiced against non-full-blood Indians or those from other tribes. This tore me apart. I realized we didn't have to worry about other people destroying us; we were going to destroy ourselves—with anger, jealousy, and disrespect for each other. This was a real turning point for me, toward the work I'm doing now.

I began to know that I wanted a better life for my children and myself. My husband and I had built a log house twelve miles from town. My husband was alcoholic, and I felt very isolated. I also missed the reservation and the Indian people. Commuting to Spokane to attend the university was difficult, so I moved back to Tacoma and began looking for ways to be with Indian people. I became very close with five Indian women whom I met there. We prayed weekly, did fund-raisers, and formed a little church that combined Indian traditions with Catholic ways. We held services, did funerals, helped with marriages and baptisms, and generally supported each other in our hopes and dreams.

In October 1991, we opened a center in Tacoma for the urban Indians. About 35 percent of them are from the streets, and the rest are urban Indians either new to the area, going to school, or working. Many wonderful things happen at our center, but our major purpose is to help people wake up to who they are and the rich heritage they have. Recognizing the spirit within can help people take responsibility for themselves, their families, the community, and then the rest of the world.

Now and then, I think of moving back to Minnesota, but I know I need to stay in Washington because the urban Indians really need me. I also realize that if I went back now, I would be seen as an outsider on the reservation. This would be a major obstacle for me in the work I want to do.

Looking back on my upbringing, I can begin to understand where some of my attitudes come from. For instance, the first time I heard my dad speak derogatorily about a black man, I couldn't believe it. I asked him, "How can you be prejudiced against someone because of their skin color, after all the prejudice you've been through?" He said, "I've never been a victim of prejudice." In his eyes, he was white, and we were 100 percent assimilated. I didn't feel close to him, as I did to my mother. She was very supportive and attended a lot of Indian things with me. She even learned to speak Chippewa. My father also spoke Chippewa, but he would not teach it to anyone else, not even when asked. Knowing something about my father's upbringing, I can understand why he had problems with drinking and was an angry, abusive man. There was shame there. When I graduated from college, my dad stopped contact with me. That was hard, but I realized one of the reasons we struggled so much with our relationship was that I had attained what he had wanted for himself but could not have because of the era when he grew up.

I wonder what it would do to a child like my father to be taken away from his family and sent to a boarding school for three, eight, twelve years. At first kids were sent to school eight hours a day, until an Indian agent wrote a memo that said, "What good is it doing us to take these little heathens into our environment to civilize them, then send them back to tepees, hunting, fishing, to live like heathens again?" The children were no longer able to speak their language, eat their traditional foods, pray in their native way, or see their families. Where were the role models to learn how to be brother, sister, husband, father, mother?

All of us children were baptized Catholic, even though my father hated Catholics. I went to many different churches; I'd go anywhere someone would take me in, give me a meal or some clothes, and maybe send me to a bible camp. Father John Haskel was the first person to tell me to be an Indian and really look into my background. I helped him write a book showing how the Indian ways mesh with Catholicism. He took me to spiritual workshops where the singing and prayers and health workshops focused on healing yourself. It was an exciting time for me and for Indian people. Many people started studying Indian society and began to see how healthy it was.

When I went back to school in 1986, I was amazed at how many people were actually studying Indian society. Before I knew it, I had made a commitment to attend a sun dance, a Native American ceremony that requires a year of preparation. The first one I attended was a four-day ritual at Mount Hood. I was mentored for a year before I actually participated. I went into a real spiritual high, which lasted for months and months. It really seemed to fill a need I had.

One of the key things I learned during this time (and the hardest for me to handle) was to look for the positive in everything. It's a negative world out there, and it's real easy to find the negative. I had to completely clean up my life: drinking, smoking, caffeine, eating a healthy diet, and learning to fast one day at a time.

The ceremony lasted many days and consisted of a process that emptied my mind, body, and soul. At the end, I was filled with spiritual food, which for me was amazing and lifesaving. I realized there is a rhythm for everything. There is a rhythm for me, and I'm part of a natural cycle. Things are happening in my life for a reason I may not understand now, but I will someday.

Father John Haskel helped me understand the role of women in our society. The woman, he says, is the healer, the life-giver, and has the power. My belief is that Indian men have suffered most. They don't know where they fit in anymore. With the man's loss of function in society came a loss of pride and sense of self-worth. I see many women today who work outside the home, take care of their families, and put up with a lot of abuse. I know probably only a handful of women who have a balance in their lives and who are in a relationship with a male companion who respects what they do outside and inside the home.

My children are the core of my life. I try to talk openly with them and include them in my life as much as possible, so that they will be aware of their heritage. When we moved from the reservation into town, my daughter told me that what she missed the most were the stars, hearing the crickets at night, and seeing the sun come up over the mountain. When she told me this, I knew I didn't have to worry about her; she was grounded, connected to nature.

I feel it's up to Indian women to keep the ball rolling and to be supportive of the men. I feel I'm using my power in a good way to break the role modeling I grew up with. I will not allow myself to be dominated by a man or to put up with abusive behavior. It's very important that we all become spiritually connected again—not just Indian men and women but *all* people.

Verna Millage lives near Ogema, Minnesota, and is an enrolled member of the White Earth Reservation. She is the mother of five children and has one adopted granddaughter. Verna earned a bachelor of science degree from Moorhead State University and has been involved in the education profession for more than two decades. Her prime concern is seeing that Indian children reach their maximum potential academically. Lowering the high school and college dropout rate of Indian students is her life's quest.

Verna Millage
Born: January 15, 1933

Our home was filled with music when I was growing up. I can still see all the guitars, banjos, and violins hung on one wall of our old house. My mom played the harmonica. A long time ago, it seemed that Indian people wanted to be musicians. I know a lot of Indian people who play musical instruments as a hobby or just for fun, like the guitar, harmonica, or violin. I remember so many evenings when we would get out our instruments and play or sing. We just loved it!

My mother's family were dairy farmers who settled on the Wild Rice River. My mother talked often about driving an ox cart with twin oxen. A few years ago, some of my siblings and I drove up to Beaulieu to see my mom's old farmstead and tried to find the cemetery where her family members were buried. We didn't have much luck, though, and couldn't find any relatives' markers. Many of the Indian cemeteries were plowed under and no longer exist.

We were raised with a great deal of Indian tradition. Both my parents danced in the powwows every year, and both spoke fluent Ojibwe. I don't know where my father learned it, perhaps from my mother. I can remember waking up in the morning and hearing the two of them talking in Ojibwe. We kids did learn some of the language, but you have to use it to retain it. I took two quarters of it at Moorhead State, and much of it did come back. It's a difficult language to learn. We were all given Indian names, but I no longer remember mine.

Every year we would take part in the wild rice harvest festival at Nay-tah-waush. It's part of our Indian culture and tradition. When the ricing season is done, there is a big feast and powwow. I still go there every year. My parents riced on Big Rice Lake. We would camp out there and stay until the ricing was done. I can remember my parents doing all the harvesting themselves. They had a big kettle, and mom fanned the rice with a birch-bark fan. My dad treaded it, which was like dancing on it. They did it entirely the traditional way.

This festival celebrated the harvest of all crops because many Indian people have gardens. Another traditional part of Indian life is maple sugaring. My mother made maple sugar every year. We had our own maple-sugar bush about five or six miles from home. We used to walk up there carrying our supplies, like the big kettle. My mother boiled the sap out there, making gallons of maple syrup. My mother stored and canned everything. When my brothers went hunting, my mother canned the deer meat and stored it in the cellar. When I think about it now, it is something I miss.

My dad had an old radio that we would listen to in the evenings. We also did a lot of visiting with relatives. We'd pack up and go five, ten, fifteen miles down the road to visit. Sometimes we'd stay overnight and play games with the other kids, swim in the river near Rice Lake, and share a meal. It was so much fun! These things aren't done much anymore.

My parents were very religious and made us go to church, sometimes twice a day. We got up in the morning and went to the Episcopal church, where we had all been baptized. Then on Wednesday and Sunday evenings, we went to the Gospel Alliance Church in Nay-tah-waush. I can still sing all those songs by heart. The religion and faith my parents taught us were very important in learning values. Kids need something to believe in, some rules and guidelines.

I spent my four high school years at the Flandreau Indian School in South Dakota. It's funny, but a couple of other people from Nay-tah-waush and I got on the bus without even having our names on the list. We had our suitcases, but no papers. We weren't thinking, "What if we get there and aren't accepted?" In the end, they let us in. I loved the school, but it had its pros and cons. Much of it was very pleasant, but we missed not being able to practice our culture. I feel as though I learned a lot of things that helped me later in life. It gave me a determination to get an education that I probably wouldn't have had back home. I sometimes hear people say negative things about Flandreau, but I usually defend it by saying, "Well, if not for Flandreau, I probably wouldn't have graduated." In many ways, being at Flandreau was like being in the army. There was a time regimen that I still practice today. I think they did not promote the Indian traditions because nine different tribes were there. How could they use nine different languages? I decided to become a teacher because both the school and my mother were encouraging that. I think there was only one Indian teacher at the school and two black teachers, who were really nice to us. The instructors were a major positive influence.

After graduating from the Flandreau School, I got married and had five children. I lost one son, in 1979. My husband and I divorced, and he died a short time later. As a single parent of five children in the 1960s, I knew I didn't want to be on welfare. I was going to Detroit Lakes every day to clean houses. My self-esteem and self-confidence were really low. One day Frank Annette, who worked at the employment office in Detroit Lakes, gave me a dose of reality therapy. He had a talk with me about going back to school and bettering myself. I asked for his help, and he got me signed up for school that very day. I took some course work at Detroit Lakes Tech until I got sick and needed surgery. I dropped out and didn't go back, just like a lot of people on the reservation.

Under Title Four and Title Five, I got a job as home-school-coordinator liaison in Detroit Lakes. Then I went on to get the same job in Waubun, Minnesota. That's when I heard about the extension courses offered by Moorhead State University. I took a few of those courses and decided to enroll at Bemidji State University around 1975. My niece and I carpooled to Bemidji for one year, and I got really good grades. Those grades were motivating for me; they gave me the determination to continue college.

Bemidji is a long commute from Detroit Lakes, though, and I had high school kids to raise. It was hard. I needed something closer to home, so I could work and go to school. I enrolled at Moorhead State full-time during the summer and took evening and weekend external-studies classes during the school year. I took classes there for five to six years and finally graduated in 1986 with a bachelor of science degree in human services, with an emphasis on chemical-dependency counseling.

While still going to school, I was hired as the coordinator for Moorhead State University's White Earth Program. I organized classes on the reservation for nontraditional students. During that five-year period, I was in Moorhead a lot and served on several boards. Every time I turned around, someone was asking me to be on another board. Meetings, meetings! It was very good for me, though.

In 1989 I decided I was just doing too much traveling. I had adopted my young granddaughter and knew I needed to work closer to home. I also needed to pay for diapers, day care, and so on. The county was in the process of adopting her out. My son, her father, wanted me to adopt her. I tried going through the

Indian Child Welfare Act, but my granddaughter was not "Indian enough" to qualify. Under this act, Indian family members are given preference in the adoption proceedings of Indian children. I ended up hiring a lawyer and paying for the entire adoption myself.

I now work at the Circle of Life School in White Earth. I've been here for about five years as the special education and vocational education transitional instructor. A great deal of my work is with special-education children and their transition from school to work or postsecondary education. I also work with high school kids and their transition after graduation.

I took several courses about chemical dependency because I see so many people on the reservation with chemical-dependency-related problems, including students and their families. It is really a major problem with Indian people. There were chemical-dependency problems in my own family. I really wanted to help in this area, and now I teach a chemical-dependency class to seventh through ninth graders.

My main concern in the education field is seeing that kids reach their fullest potential. Out of the seventeen graduating seniors this year, only nine or ten have enrolled in postsecondary classes. I wish I could get all seventeen signed up! Often it takes a few years after graduation for the kids to figure this out. They come knocking on my door, and I help them enroll. It's hard for these kids to go on and further their education. There is a real culture shock on the campus of a big institution. The Indian retention rate for high school and college students is poor, so I work at improving this.

Life has changed so much from when I was growing up. I don't see families having time together. I also see more vandalism on the reservation. We used to leave everything out and unlocked. You can't do that anymore. The role of women has changed as well. Indian women are now going out to work instead of staying home to take care of the family. There are a lot of things we need to work on to maintain strong bonds within our families.

Eleanore Robertson

Born: April 8, 1929

Eleanore Robertson was born in the old White Earth Indian Hospital, and was raised and educated in Pine Point, Minnesota. As a child, she became interested in nursing and was influenced by a public health nurse who worked in this small community and who started a "nurses club," which Eleanore joined in the sixth grade. Eleanore is now the director for the Tucson Area Indian Health Service Office, one of twelve area offices in the United States. In 1980, she was named director for the Aberdeen Area Indian Health Service Office, and was the first Indian woman ever to hold such a position. She credits her large, supportive family for her interest in education and subsequent fifty-year career in public health. Eleanore has one daughter, who is an attorney, and two "wonderful" granddaughters. She lives in an apartment in Tucson, Arizona.

During the depression, most families in town earned their living through the WPA [Works Progress Administration]. That's how our school, our roads, and our bridges were built. But we were secure as children growing up there, and we all had a place to sleep and food to eat. I don't remember any orphans or homeless people. Someone was always there to take care of us. The community would come together when there was trouble. We were secure; our futures were up to us, whatever we wanted to do. I don't believe any of us were discouraged from thinking about college. When everyone is poor, the color of your skin doesn't matter; it's an equal playing field. The Chippewa tribe was a source of pride to us, and we all strongly identified with it.

When we finished eighth grade, my classmates and I went to high school in Park Rapids for two years. We were all bussed to school, but no one got concerned about that. At that time, we were integrated with all the other kids from the small towns in the area and had a chance to compete in the mainstream.

But then it seemed as though the community changed overnight. I'll never forget it. We were all listening to the radio when we heard that Pearl Harbor had been bombed. Everyone left to join the service, Indian and non-Indian. Those who stayed back were the elderly folks and the children. My mother took a job at the sanatorium in Walker, Minnesota, where I finished high school. In the summer of 1945, I went to Chicago to stay with a cousin. I had never been to a big city before, and it was quite an experience. My cousin worked for the BIA [Bureau of Indian Affairs], and through some of her connections I got accepted by the Haskell Institute of Lawrence, Kansas, an Indian boarding school. I didn't learn much, but I had a real good time.

I had several different jobs after that, but I knew then that I really wanted to go into nursing. My aunt was the director of nursing at the Los Angeles County Hospital; she suggested that I work as a nurse's aide for a while. I got a job in Pasadena for a year, while I attempted to get into nursing schools around the country. I was accepted at Methodist Hospital in Los Angeles, and I believe the only reason I got in was because they had never had an Indian person before. I think they expected me to fail; I had to take my basic science classes at UCLA, and my high school background was not strong. But after taking some preliminary tests, they accepted me to their three-year diploma program. The tuition was $320, which I had saved from my job as a nurse's aide, and I paid my aunt five dollars a week to live at her house. I graduated in 1949.

I have told my daughter that I do not recall ever feeling discriminated against for being Indian, nor do I remember feeling less than anyone else. If it happened, I either didn't recognize it as discrimination or didn't pay any attention to it. My identity as an Indian was established when I was young. This made it possible for me to move in and out of things easily. It was no big deal. I've always thought everybody has a fighting chance in this world. Some people have more help than others, but there is opportunity for everyone. There are ways to get things done, even today.

Although everyone thought I was crazy, I joined the army during the Korean War. It was a wonderful experience. I saw a lot of this country and met a man from Louisville, Kentucky, whom I married. For a few years, I lived in Louisville, where my daughter was born. When she was five or six months old, my husband and I came to a parting of the ways. I needed a job, so I boarded a bus and asked the driver where the nearest hospital was. He said, "At Third and Oak, you'll find Norton." I found the hospital, got hired, and went to work the next day. I stayed in Louisville until 1975.

I began to think about going back to school on the GI Bill. One day my daughter and I were walking down the street, and I saw a dog that had been hit by a car. This was right in front of Nazareth College, a Catholic school for women. I went in to call the Humane Society about the dog, and while I was there, I decided I might as well enroll for school. After five years of scrimping and saving on part-time pay, I got my bachelor's degree in nursing. Then I taught at Norton for ten years and got my master's degree in education administration at the same time.

My family and friends kept encouraging me to move back closer to home and work for Indian Health Services. I finally decided to do that and was hired as a hospital nurse-consultant in the Aberdeen area. This is the first time I can remember that anybody asked me about being Indian. I said, "You don't want to know if I'm Indian or not; you want to know if I'm a capable person who can do the job well." They said, "No, we have to have a DIB." "What's that?" I asked. They said, "Degree of Indian blood." So I called White Earth and got this piece of paper that confirmed me as an enrolled member of the Chippewa Indian Tribe. That's how I got to South Dakota.

While I was working there, the area directorship opened up. I thought I could do that job, so I applied for it. Everyone was aghast! No Indian woman had ever applied for this job before—and a nurse besides! No one dreamed I would get the job, and if I did, I would never be able to do it. Women can't do those jobs! A tribal chairman, who reminded me that a woman couldn't do this job, interviewed me. I reminded *him* that men certainly hadn't handled it very well; they had been through three male directors in three years.

Aberdeen was a tough area. I got a taste of politics. I also became reacquainted with relatives and friends in the area. This was lucky for me because from time to time I really needed their support. I had made a recommendation that area directors should be rotated, that they should not stay in one place too long. So I was asked to go and assess a research program, to make some changes, and perhaps to shut it down. It was *not* fun. I had to reorganize and downgrade it and take on the governing body. Like Harry Truman said, "The buck stops here." I had to have the courage of my convictions. I was fortunate to have my family and good friends there.

Years ago I had taken a course at Purdue University. Another woman and I were asked at that time to get into this management program—maybe as guinea pigs. We had to confront many attitudes and mind-sets about women's issues. I finished the program and got a certificate. This was one of the best things I ever did, besides getting my master's degree in education administration and a minor in guidance and counseling. I think this prepared me better than an MBA.

The most important things I have learned to prepare for this job are how to deal with people, how to confront conflict, and how to handle crime issues. I've had men cry in my office; I've handed them a tissue and waited until they were ready to talk about the problem. Then I went home and cried later. I've shed plenty of tears, and I've learned to control the urge at times to sock somebody in the nose.

Being a woman in management was not always easy, but I think I have always felt confident that I knew my job. I was a nurse. I knew health care. I also learned that men have the same weaknesses and fears that women have. I've always tried to treat all people with respect. I also love to tell jokes, laugh, and have a good time. A sense of humor really helps.

Sometimes I wish I had finished my degrees faster, but then I think about it and decide I wouldn't change a thing. I've had a good time, met wonderful people, laughed a lot, and always got a big kick out of life. I am not spending any time on regrets.

Natalie was born and raised in Detroit Lakes, Minnesota. Her mother is Scandinavian, and her father is Indian, enrolled at White Earth. Natalie feels her life has been influenced by her heritage, by growing up poor in a racist community, and by a dream she had as a young adult that showed her how to help her people. She is presently the director of the Anishinabe Center in Detroit Lakes and has applied for a Bush Foundation grant that would enable her to pursue a master's degree. She is the mother of three children and soon will become a grandmother. A respected activist in her community, Natalie boldly confronts issues of racism and perseveres in helping her people heal, a process she considers critical to improving their lives.

Natalie Ann Greenlaw
Born: August 20, 1956

There is a definite significance to the railroad tracks in Detroit Lakes, where I grew up. Most of the Indian people and the poor people lived on the north side of the tracks. I lived on the north side of town until I graduated from high school. My mother was divorced and raised me and my older brother alone until she married my stepfather, when I was about ten years old. She had two sons in this marriage. I am very close to my brothers, especially the oldest one because we were closer in age; I was a teenager when my two younger brothers were born.

Elementary school was the most turbulent time for me. I was growing up and trying to sort out who I was. I was a McDougall, which in my town meant you were Indian, but I had blonde hair and blue eyes. My mother was divorced, and we were very poor. What did all this mean? I often felt that I did not have a place where I fit in. Most people I knew in school seemed to have a "box" that defined them. I didn't have that, and it was confusing.

Add to this the fact that I wasn't a fabulous student and didn't like school very much. I started experimenting with drugs and alcohol at a very young age, and in senior high school, I became addicted to alcohol. When I think back to those high school days, my recollection is vague. I was very confused.

I didn't know there was a disease called alcoholism until I was thirty-two years old. When I learned about it, I realized that most of my father's family were alcoholic. Many are recovering now, but many are dead. It was just a way of life when I was growing up. Naturally, I married a man who was also alcoholic, and when that marriage dissolved, I began to see the big picture. Realizing that there is a disease called alcoholism helped me set my path and decide where I wanted to go with my life. I had three beautiful children from my marriage, and I knew I didn't want them to go through the things that I did during my younger years. I made a conscious choice to change my life and got involved in a recovery program. I've been sober now for about five years.

I believe now that alcoholism is a symptom of deeper underlying issues. I did not have a strong sense of self. I think children need to feel they fit in somewhere to feel secure, to have a sense of likeness and similarity. I didn't have that. I always felt very isolated, alone, and different. I think this contributed to my depression, which made me a prime candidate for self-medication.

Growing up as I did, I began to believe that I was not in control of my own life, that whatever happened, happened, and that a person just had to figure things out as life happened to them. This can be a curse or a blessing. I am probably a stronger person now having survived this, but I did not learn many skills because of this belief.

Planning for my future and decision making were hard for me, but I knew I wanted something different for my kids. This was my motivation: to find a new way for myself and them. At the same time, I believe that each of us has a journey and that parents shouldn't try too hard to make life easier for their children. From my own experience, I can say that the hardest knocks have been the best lessons for me, and I don't want to deprive my children of these lessons. I share knowledge and bits of wisdom with them, but ultimately they have to make their own decisions and create their own pathway.

I have wondered why some children can come through all kinds of hardship and catastrophes and still reach their potential and why others don't. The answer for me is that I always felt my mother and my father loved me and gave me the freedom to develop into my own self, whatever that turned out to be. In our heritage, the belief is that you celebrate the journey of life from birth until death, and whatever paths your children choose to take, you embrace them and support them along the way.

Even though I appreciate the culture of my ancestors now, I didn't as a child. In my family, it was not good to be Indian. My dad, my uncles, and my grandpa all had only an eighth-grade education, so they were laborers. In our town, it was very difficult to get work if you looked Indian. I remember my family trying to figure out ways to look less Indian. So I saw the downside of being Indian. But I also learned about traditional ways of life in the neighborhood where I grew up, and I'm grateful for that. I saw the richness of both cultures. I remember that when my friends and I would go to the local grocery to buy candy, I was the only one who was allowed to go behind the counter to pick out my candy. The others were made to wait on the other side and put their pennies on the counter. At the time, I didn't make the connection between my lighter skin and blonde hair and the way I was treated in some situations. I figured out much later that I could play both sides of the fence. I was in my early twenties when I began to accept my mixed heritage and be proud of it.

Higher education was not expected of my family members. But when I decided to make some changes in my life, I started to consider college. At this time I had a powerful, clear dream. My dream showed me the Anishinabe Center, and it became apparent to me what I was supposed to do. I tried to work on this idea, but it was a huge failure. I couldn't get anyone to support me. And why should they? I was this whacked-out woman with no credentials and a grand dream!

At this point, I became very angry and decided to do it myself. I needed guidance, and I thought of Verna Millage, the mother of a good friend of mine. Verna had gone back to school as an older-than-average student, and I thought she could show me the way. When I called her, she was working at Moorhead State. She said, "Come on up. I'll help you with the process." I was scared to death, but I went and was lovingly accepted into Verna's office, where she helped me fill out the forms and get started. Before long I had a focus, a direction. I knew the degree I needed and what I wanted to do. So then I began five years of commuting a hundred miles each day, raising three kids, and working full-time. It was brutal, but I knew that in five years I would be where I wanted to be. If I hadn't had the dream to show me the way and motivate me, I never would have been able to do it.

I am still working toward my dream. It gets very discouraging at times, but I know in my heart from my experiences that the Anishinabe culture is rich and beautiful. The center serves as a cultural-outreach resource. We promote a way of life called the Red Road. We encourage the learning of our language, our customs, our ceremonies, and all the traditional things that have been lost over the years. If people can get in touch with this and begin to appreciate and respect who they are and where they have come from, they will be able to improve their lives. Everywhere I look I see these wonderful, interesting, beautiful people in my life who are suffering and hurting. They are drunks. They are unemployed. And I see now, through my life and my education, that this is so because of all of the self-hate in their hearts. Because I grew up with racism and continue to see it, I know it is very hurtful.

I'm hoping that this year there may be a kind of shift in the perspective of the community, its people, and its agencies, so that Indian families might begin to be viewed differently and to receive fair and equal treatment. We are trying to buy an old school in town so that we can provide anything a family could possibly need—from recreation to spiritual guidance to school tutoring to job readiness. We would like an emergency shelter there for homeless people, as well as transitional housing for those who need it. We also hope to incorporate stronger traditional perspectives in treatment programs. Our dreams are big, but our vision is clear.

I consider my generation a "recovery generation." Our elders say it will take about five generations for our people to recover from the trauma of the boarding-school era. When the children were taken away, we became lost souls, lost spirits. Our community is beginning to look at some of the reasons we have a "north side" and a "south side" in our town. We are beginning to see the damage we do to families when we hold on to those beliefs and misunderstandings. My hope is that our children will continue the work we've started so the restoration can take place, even though I won't see it in my lifetime.

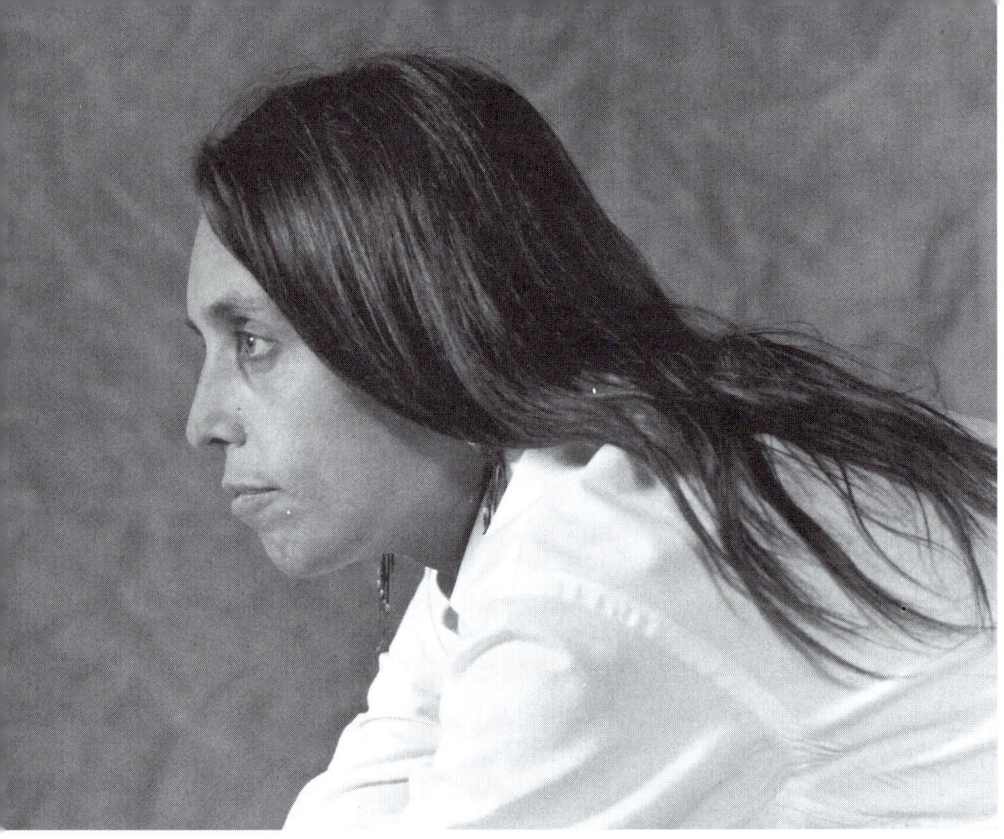

Winona LaDuke

Born: August 18, 1959

Winona LaDuke is known regionally and nationally as an activist and supporter of Native American rights, women, and the environment. Winona is a board member of Greenpeace USA and executive director of the White Earth Land Recovery Project. She was the running mate of candidate Ralph Nader in the 1996 presidential election. She was born in Los Angeles to a biracial couple; her mother is a Russian Jew and her father was Native American, enrolled at White Earth. She spent her early childhood in a Mexican-American community and moved to Ashland, Oregon, a place she remembers at that time as being racist and conservative. She also recalls that she was "never picked for teams, never asked to things, and didn't have a date to the junior/senior prom." Winona credits her family and their strong interest in current events and issues of justice with starting her down the road of political activism. "If you see something that you think is wrong, speak out," they often told her. Winona is largely home-schooling her two young children. She is also the author of the recently published novel *Last Standing Woman*.

One of my core beliefs is that the *whole* community is responsible for its future—not just a tribe, a church, or a certain faction in the community. My childhood on the West Coast exposed me to various kinds of prejudice, not just racial. For example, my mother was a divorced woman, a fact that carried its own stigma in the early sixties. When we moved to Ashland, we were near the Klamath Reservation. This reserved land had been terminated about ten years before we moved there; that meant the government took all the land (including the forests), paid the tribe members with cash settlements, and said they weren't Indians anymore! I recall a lot of racism.

My mother and stepfather still live there. My mother just retired as an art professor and an artist. My stepfather is an entomologist; his heritage is Norwegian. My biological father passed away about three years ago. Incidentally, the last time I went to vote at White Earth, I found out he was listed as having voted in the previous election, although he was deceased at the time. I'm familiar with election problems. My father's name was Vincent LaDuke, and he was known as Sun Bear. He was an author, and when I was young he sometimes was an extra in Western movies. My memory is that he became a kind of religious and spiritual leader in a New Age movement. I believe this is one reason why my parents did not stay together: my mother did not want to do that.

My father was quite active politically in the Indian community on the West Coast and in Nevada, and my mother was active in the antiwar and civil rights movements. On speaking tours, I've had people come up to me who remembered my folks on a picket line with them. I came from a family of strong values and good political stock, so when people ask me why I think the way I do, I really have to credit my family.

While I was in high school, my speech teacher really encouraged me. The debate team in our little town took the state title six years in a row. I wasn't an intellectual or a jock, but I *was* good at giving speeches. And my parents had raised me to go off and "do the right thing." So speech was a natural. I had things to say.

I went east to Harvard after high school, and there were only about seven Indians in my class. We hung out together, and I had the opportunity to hear some excellent speakers. Some of what they said really resonated with me because I was at a point in my life when I was trying to sort things out, figure out who I was. This was really a wonderful time. I remember interviewing a fellow student, the director of the National Indian Treaty Council, for a paper I was writing. We talked about Indian issues, and he said there is no such thing as an Indian problem; instead, it is a problem with society in general. This conversation changed my perspective from feeling like a victim to knowing there was a structural problem that needed work. I was fine, but my frame of reference had changed. After this I worked with the Navajo for about a year and then worked in South Dakota for a while. I came home in 1983.

When I got out of college, I became the principal of the Circle of Life School. It was a total fiasco! I guess they figured if I graduated from Harvard I could be a principal. I was twenty-three. I was not suited to be supervised by the people in charge at that time. My experience is not in structured authority and administration—my gift is in working with people to use their ideas about language and culture and to teach in innovative ways.

I was there six months and then went back to grad school at MIT [Massachusetts Institute of Technology] for a year. When I returned, I was totally involved with the nonprofit private sector. It was not an easy situation, and at times I would become very frustrated at the slow progress. But things take as long as they take. It is a character flaw of mine to become impatient. That's also one reason I work at the national level. I cannot *demand* that the tribal government work with us, so I also work in other communities around the country that need help and appreciate what we do. I would probably be much more effective if I could remain singularly focused, but that's not my nature. If I can't make something change at the rate that I want it to change, then I need to do something else for a while.

It is important for me to take time to feed my soul, like being with my horses, participating in ceremonies, or dancing. Seeing Indian women striving to accomplish things that will help our people feeds my soul. It encourages me to see women standing up for their children and what they believe in, resisting government help, and holding on to their beliefs with dignity. That also feeds my soul.

Sometimes the work I do gets very frustrating and wearisome. When this happens, I need to diversify. For example, I plan to go to school soon to study Ojibwe. I feel my future lies in the area where I am now living, so it would help to know the language. I feel I owe a great debt to our community because I've been given a lot of gifts in my life. I believe it is my responsibility to share what I have in the best way I can. I rely greatly on a spiritual power. I pray a lot. I feel that I am only a little speck in the universe, and I try to make the best decisions I can to use the gifts I have.

Right now, in addition to my work at the White Earth Land Recovery Project, I'm doing national political-advocacy work on environmental issues. I run the project for a Native American foundation called Seventh Generation Fund. We raise money for groups nationally and then distribute it in the form of grants to small groups. On the national level, this work includes an organization called Honor the Earth. The Indigo Girls give concerts to help us raise money; last year we raised $250,000.

Cultivating leadership in the Indian community is another primary interest of mine. We have a severe leadership crisis. One reason for this may be that the governmental systems we inherited are alien to our culture and don't work well. Traditionally, we have had our own systems. I am a board member of the Indigenous Women's Network, which works to increase the volume and visibility of native women in our communities. Young women are identified and then participate in an eighteen-month mentorship program. After they are trained, they are sent out to work for a foundation or for tribal government.

I believe this community has a wealth of women who have done amazing things—not only here but also in Minneapolis and across the country. Their achievements are so underrecognized, yet one can see that changes are being made.

I'm grateful for my Harvard education, but I must say I learned most of the things I know from community people. The things I have learned experientially from them have at least equal value with my formal education. Because of this, I'm home-schooling my children. We have high expectations for the children in our household. We have many guests in our house, and my children learn from all of them. We celebrate differences.

Marilyn Thelen
Born: March 17, 1952

Marilyn Thelen and her husband are partners in a drugstore in Mahnomen, Minnesota; she is the business manager and marketing person. Marilyn was born and raised in Mahnomen, but she has lived in many different places with her family while running various businesses. Marilyn is happy to be settled again in her home area, where she pursues many interests and, with her husband, raises their three children.

I was eight years old, living on a farm near Mahnomen with my parents and three siblings, when my father died. My mother moved us into town and went to work for an attorney, whom she married several years later. We children all went to school there, and I graduated from Mahnomen High School in 1970. My mother had four more children in her new marriage. My maiden name was Gish.

After graduation I went to college at St. Cloud State and St. Catherine's, in St. Paul. I got married during my third year of college and moved with my husband to Perham, Minnesota, where he began his career in pharmacy with the St. Mary's Hospital satellite location there.

We've lived in a lot of places and done a wide spectrum of things. For example, I taught piano while I was raising our three small children. We went into the retail pharmacy business in a store in Piers, Minnesota, a small town near Little Falls. Anytime I've been in a business role with my husband, I've basically been the manager—in charge of the employees, the buying, and the operations in what you might call the front end of the store. In 1987 we sold that store and moved to Fargo, where my husband tried another career direction and I went to college at Moorhead State University. There was such a large gap in my education that I left school and went to work for the VA hospital temporarily while we figured out what we were going to do. We were the owners of a drugstore in the Moorhead Center Mall when my husband got a call from St. Mary's in Detroit Lakes asking him to come back as director of the pharmacy. In 1992 we had arranged financing to purchase the drugstore in Mahnomen, and we have been here ever since. Now we live next door to my parents, and it feels good, much more settled. This is where my roots are, and I hope my children can feel that, too.

My family is very close; perhaps the death of my father when we children were quite young caused us to rely on each other and become a close-knit family. My mother was enrolled at White Earth, and my father was of German-Dutch descent. I don't believe I was really aware as a child that I was of Native American descent. It was something we never talked about. I knew my grandmother looked Native American, but that's as far as it went in our family. I don't recall any race issues at school either. When I was a junior in high school, I was called out of class one day by my counselor to see if I wanted to join the Amerind Club. It made me feel singled out to be asked in this way, and I felt it would separate me from the rest of my friends, so I didn't join.

My grandmother was a descendant of Native Americans who came down from Canada and settled in a little village east of here called Beaulieu. They were instrumental in the fur trade between the Indians and the white people. When I was young, we visited the gravesites of my ancestors on Madeline Island. My grandmother was a proud woman, proud of her ancestry, but she didn't talk about it very openly. Even so, many of her Native American values have been passed down. For example, we value the family highly. Grandmother is ninety-three years old now and lives by herself in town. She is a calm, serene woman who shares things about her life with us, but she never offers a lot. It was a quiet pride that we picked up.

My brother Brent is extremely interested in our heritage. He actually served on the RTC [Reservation Tribal Council] years ago. My two older brothers were enrolled a long time ago, but after that the rolls were closed for some time, and there was a lot of confusion about qualifying for enrollment. I was finally enrolled in 1991, when the rolls were opened again.

My grandfather's ancestry is a bit uncertain. Brent has done research and found information saying that he was Native American, even though this is not indicated on his birth certificate. So I am probably more Native American than what my birth certificate shows.

My own son, who is an artist, became interested in our heritage when he spent a weekend talking with other Native American artists at the Red Lake Reservation. At that time, he read the book *Black Elk Speaks,* which furthered his interest. He has worked on some projects that involved talking with Native Americans and getting their opinions on current issues and problems. He has a lot of pride in his ancestry and is considering doing graduate work at the University of Arizona, where there is a Native American art program. My daughters are also showing interest in their background, and we have begun to talk more frequently about it.

My youngest daughter, Anna, has darker skin than her siblings do, and her features are more Native American. She is experiencing more issues of race than my other children did. The school is dealing with some really tough issues concerning race and harassment. Anna's teacher called me one day to report an incident where Anna had been confronted and sort of threatened. Anna had not mentioned it, and when I asked her about it, she said she knew the threats didn't mean anything. She is proud of her heritage and has a strong self-image. To my daughter, everyone is just like her; there is no real difference, no division.

I have worked hard to instill in my children self-confidence and a sense of well-being. I have tried to teach them that they are basically responsible for themselves. I have consciously tried to do this to help them feel secure because I knew it could be hard on them to move as many times as we have. All three of them are very compassionate kids.

I have had a busy life and an active career, but my children are definitely my top priority. I like my work, but I feel fortunate that I have had the freedom to take time off if my children have needed me.

My mother was Catholic and my father was Lutheran. I was raised and confirmed in the Lutheran church. My mother made sure we were active and involved in our church, but she remained Catholic the whole time. Sometimes my siblings and I would attend the Catholic church with my mother on holidays and special occasions. I took classes in Catholicism after I met my future husband, and I converted to that faith before we were married. All four of us children ended up in different religious denominations. I guess I would say that I'm a very spiritual person and so are my brothers, but religion is secondary to spirituality.

Experiencing the loss of loved ones when I was growing up definitely shaped my life. As a child, I believed that somehow I was responsible for the deaths that occurred in our family. I know children often reason that something they have done wrong has caused the painful loss. After my sister died, however, I was older and realized that it couldn't be my fault, that God was not punishing me. I began digging deeper into spirituality and the meaning of life.

I have not been as active in reservation ceremonies and tribal issues as my brother has. I play a much more removed role, in the background. I try to be involved only in places where I feel I can make a difference: my home, the church, and the American Cancer Society. But I am very interested, supportive, and aware of what is going on. I have watched my brother, who is an educator, handle accusations of favoritism toward Native American students. I'm convinced that whatever is talked about at home is carried to school with the child. If children were taught at home that we are all one, that we are all the same, there would be fewer incidents of hate and suspicion.

Besides these interests of home and family, I also enjoy art and music. I am not an accomplished pianist and do not enjoy playing in public; I still play strictly for my own enjoyment. I am a private person and enjoy spending time by myself—reading, working on the computer, cooking, and, most recently, developing an interest in landscaping and gardening.

My career in business has always been interesting and challenging. I believe there will always be a place for a small pharmacy in a community, despite the trends of mail order, HMOs [health maintenance organizations], and mass merchandisers, because we provide personal service.

I believe that all the experiences one has in life are just learning tools. We are who we are today because of what happened in the past. I enjoy my life and its challenges, and I enjoy living in Mahnomen. I really want to stay here—living in this community as a Native American, raising a family, and being happy on the reservation. I'm glad I am where I am right now.

Myrna Smith is a nurse at the White Earth Clinic who enjoys working with patients and is especially interested in public health. Myrna was born and raised in the Nay-tah-waush area. Her father traveled as a foreman for a road-construction company and would take his whole family and other Nay-tah-waush families with him to the job sites; Myrna recalls her family living like "gypsies" during this period. She is one of five children and also has two stepbrothers and one stepsister. Myrna's first husband died from a heart attack at age forty-one, when their children were teenagers. Her second husband has multiple health problems. Myrna enjoys working as a health-care provider and expects to continue in her career indefinitely; she wonders if there really are any "golden years." She also delights in her grandchildren.

Myrna Joyce Smith
Born: May 14, 1941

Myrna Joyce Smith

I have been a nurse since 1972. I went to work initially because I needed more independence; I hated having to ask my husband for money. When my youngest child was in first grade, I decided to pursue a nursing career. This was something I had wanted to do since I was five years old and a patient at Gillette Children's Hospital in St. Paul being treated for severe burns. I went to LPN [licensed practical nurse] school in Detroit Lakes and later worked at the detox center in White Earth. I took my RN [registered nurse] training at St. Luke's in Fargo. I graduated and realized this would always be a part of my life. After all these years, I still feel like I *need* to work at my profession. It is very important to me.

I was going to nursing school in Fargo when my husband became very sick. I would drive home at night and see to his needs. I don't think people realize how difficult it is to be a caregiver twenty-four hours a day. It can really take its toll. This was the hardest part of my education. I stuck with it, though, because it was interesting, and I really enjoyed working with people and the challenge of the program. The only difficult thing for me was being an Indian person. I have always felt uncomfortable with a whole lot of people. I am not sure why, even now. Some people call it being "Indianonish." It is just a feeling of preferring to stand in the back. I guess I am not the only one who feels this way, or they wouldn't have a name for it. It's probably part of our culture, or maybe that's just the way some people are. But I can function well at work. I can chair meetings, and I am the coordinator of the diabetics program.

I didn't learn much about our culture as a kid growing up. I recall that being Indian was looked down upon. My grandparents spoke Ojibwe, for example, and my mother was raised with it; but in school they didn't let them speak their language. My mother says the reason she quit school was because she didn't have the right clothes. But I suspect there was something more than that.

I loved my grandparents very much. They spoke the language, and they took me to powwows. I remember as a child dancing with my grandmother in these ceremonies. My mom said that her parents used to practice Midewiwin, but they turned to Christianity later and became Episcopalians. I've been Episcopalian ever since I was born. My family is really quite religious. I do know people who practice some of the traditional ceremonies, but my husband and I are more comfortable in the Christian beliefs that we grew up with. Even my grandparents, whom I was so close to and who practiced the traditional ways, did not teach them to me. I think my parents thought we children would be disadvantaged in our lives if we followed the traditional ways, so they did not encourage it. Today I can say I am proud of being Indian. I just don't remember my parents talking about our heritage very much.

Last year my fifteen-year-old grandson was murdered. This was so hard for all of us. He was shot and killed. This is still really hard for us, because it doesn't seem that anything was done about it. When an Indian child is killed, it seems to me, nothing is done. Nobody ever pays. It appears that most people don't care.

Violence is a big problem in our community. We hope that the changes being made in law enforcement can be fair and equal to all people. Many are afraid the reservation might end up with *political* law enforcement, but that is not justice. Nobody wants a "goon squad." But I see the vandalism, gang activity, and violence in general getting worse. It's never been an easy life here, but at least we didn't have to lock our doors or put fences up when I was a child.

I have been a nurse at this clinic since 1980. While I was working, I also managed to take classes at Bemidji State University for my bachelor of science in nursing. I worked full-time while I did that, and I am proud of this accomplishment. The classes were not easy, and I drove 106 miles round trip to attend. Sometimes I wonder what motivated me. I guess I have always wanted to better myself, so I keep on dreaming and doing more things.

I finished my course work—all night classes—in three years and got a degree in 1993. My support person was an old friend who presently is the postmistress at Nay-tah-waush. She kept encouraging me and helped me through many, many hard times when I needed somebody.

What really keeps me going is that I know the reservation needs more nurses who are Native American. I would like to help improve this situation so that patients would feel more comfortable and relaxed when they come into the clinic. I would like to be a part of this. I have a lot of ideas about how to make this clinic a more welcoming, safe place for the patients. There are so many approaches to medicine, but they all start with the patients' feeling trust and confidence in the people who are helping them.

When my husband began having medical problems, we tried lots of things, including traditional medicine. My elderly mother-in-law knows about "black medicine water." She has helped a lot of people, but she won't tell the secret of the potion. I know that my mother-in-law gets the basis of this medicine from a root in the swamp, but she won't reveal what or where it is. It was a big red root, and it was in the swamp. I swear I will get it out of her before she goes. I believe it is something we need to know about. We need to be open-minded about a lot of approaches.

We have a beautiful new medical facility now, because our clientele was so large and continued to grow when the casino was built. The old clinic couldn't handle them all. We have four physicians, and they are all excellent. We also have one nurse practitioner, seven RNs, and two LPNs. Only two of us are enrolled at White Earth.

The health care is free to people living on the reservation. Sorting out all these rules and guidelines can get complicated. Basically we help people figure out how to get to the next step. Sometimes we have to refer patients to another facility, but we never turn anybody away who is in a critical emergency, even non-Indians. Sometimes it gets touchy and people get angry with the bureaucracy. It is also becoming more and more complicated because of intermarriages. In our clinic, it is really no longer possible to accept someone's word about being "so-and-so's grandson" without some kind of proof.

I have self-doubts at times and wonder why I worked so hard for my education. I ask myself if my education really made any difference. I've always had to work twice as hard as someone else does to prove myself. And then I question the worth of it all. But it does make a difference for me to know that I have pushed forward in what I believed. I guess that's what counts.

Michelle Lea Bellanger-Azure is a full-time student at Moorhead State University, pursuing a degree in computer science information systems. She recently won a prestigious 3M scholarship and works as a part-time bookkeeper. Michelle is a widow and the mother of two daughters. Moving to a large city and creating a successful career are important goals in her life. She is an enrolled member of the White Earth Reservation.

Michelle Lea Bellanger Azure
Born: October 21, 1966

My father was killed in a car accident when I was a child. This left my mother with three children: my older brother, my younger sister, and me. Later Mother remarried and had three more daughters. Bellanger is my biological father's name, and Azure is my married name.

    I attended Mahnomen public schools until I was sixteen. Mahnomen High School was very racially divided between the Native American students and the white students, but Nay-tah-waush Elementary had nearly all Native American students. I went to Mahnomen, and I was one of only two Native American students in the class. It's hard for two groups to integrate at this age. I knew a lot of my Indian and non-Indian friends didn't like each other. It was like I had to choose what side I was going to be on. I chose the Native American side. The school wasn't a very good place, and it wasn't fair. They judged the whole bunch on a few bad apples. I didn't feel I was learning the things I needed to learn. And I had always known how important education was.

    When I was fourteen, I became pregnant and had my daughter Tara. I told my mother, "I'm keeping this baby." I've always gotten along really well with my mother. She was very supportive of me and helped me in whatever way she could. She bought me a trailer and parked it in the same yard where she and my grandmother lived. My youngest sister was born at the same time, so for Mother it was like taking care of twins while I went to school. I dropped out of high school in January of my junior year, at age sixteen, and moved to Detroit Lakes with my daughter. I had to apply to the governor of Minnesota to get special permission to go to vocational school because I was so young. This was mostly for financial aid purposes. I got my GED [graduate equivalency degree] and went to the vo-tech in Detroit Lakes for two years. I graduated with an accounting degree and moved to Moorhead when I was eighteen.

    Lois Olson was an important mentor for me. She was the Indian education coordinator. I knew what I had to do, and she steered me on the right path. She had a small drive-in fast-food place, and I worked for her one summer. I visited with her a lot, and I knew her from school, where she was the mediator between students and administration. I trusted her and explained to her what I wanted to do. She took me to Detroit Lakes and helped me find an apartment. She helped me with the whole school process. I knew I needed a good education to support Tara and myself. I wanted a good life for us.

I married Tara's father when I was twenty, and he was twenty-two. We had two daughters and had moved to Fargo, North Dakota, when he was killed in a snowmobile accident. Now I thought I needed to get to work instead of going to school so I could take care of my daughters.

My first job in Fargo was with a CPA firm. That boss taught me so much about business practices. I had learned the fundamentals in school, but he taught me how to apply them. It was a good job, but it didn't pay much. Good experience doesn't pay the bills. So I went to work nights at K-Mart to save on day-care costs. I started as a checker, moved to customer services, and then to the cash cage. That last spot was definitely not a "people" job: I worked in one small dark room with a little window, and I wasn't happy.

Next I went to work for a window-distributing company, but that didn't last long, and then I went back to my first job for a while. I was at Coldwell Banker in the property-management division when I got word that my brother had been killed in a car accident. I decided then that life is too short to stay in a job I didn't like, so I went back to school. Tara, my oldest, was now about ten, and I knew that someday I would want to help her with college. To create a better life for us, I enrolled at Moorhead State University in March 1993. Now it was school full-time, part-time bookkeeping jobs, and lots of scholarships. 3M Company awarded me a scholarship that provided mentoring, four leadership seminars per year, and one thousand dollars for each of my junior and senior years. At my first seminar, I just kept saying to myself, "This is too good to be true!" I could see my way to my dream of a bigger city, more money, and a better way of life.

I've always been a very responsible person, always taking care of other people. I'm very motivated. I can stick up for myself if I have to. Even though I wasn't the oldest, I remember caring for my brother and sisters. My siblings are not like me and have had a lot of trouble finding their way. I've been through a lot of loss. I lost my father, husband, and brother at an early age. When people ask me how I handled this, I reply that everything I've been through has made me who I am and is a part of who I am. It's not sad to me. All these things are part of my destiny. One thing I try to do for myself is work out at the gym. I used to go five days a week. I like the aerobics and cardio equipment. I'm doing things at work for my employers, things at school for my professors, and things at home for my children. This is the one small thing I can do for myself. The rewards are much better than the consequences of not going. I also like to read and usually devour a big book over Christmas vacation.

Growing up on the reservation, I knew I was Indian, but I didn't know how important that should be to me. I hadn't learned any Native American history or even recognition of it in school. We learned a little from our grandparents, but not much. After I accomplish more, I'd like to go back and study this area. I know there's a void; I just have to figure out how to fill it. One area I want to focus on is the Native American religion. I became very interested in this when I attended a four-day funeral ceremony when my uncle died. It was the most peaceful, beautiful thing I have ever experienced.

    I think the reservation is changing and that it's on a good road right now. I wish they would do more for the elders, though, and that more influential people were active in the changes. But I don't think I'll ever go back to the reservation. I don't have the desire. It is not where I want to be.

Melody LaFriniere has a Ph.D. from the University of North Dakota in counseling psychology. She was the first female American Indian game warden employed by Minnesota's Department of National Resources. Melody has held a variety of positions in the corrections and counseling fields. She has a daughter and a granddaughter, who are, she says, the motivating forces in her life. She also admits to a lifelong passion for horses.

Melody LaFriniere
Born: August 1, 1952

From what I can remember of my childhood, I've always been the odd duck. I used to think when I was a kid that I was adopted because I never fit into what my brothers and sisters did. They were hell-raisers, like a lot of the kids on reservation, but I never wanted to play. I always had my face in a book. I wanted something more or something different; I just didn't know what it was. Maybe it was the era. This was 1969, 1970, when things were changing anyway, and maybe I just got caught up in the independence of that time. Or maybe I was just different.

I remember that school was not encouraged. It was expected, when we reached the age of sixteen, that we'd drop out. We were never expected to graduate. Just when I was sensing that I was different, I was assured at school that I would never amount to anything. I remember the counselor in high school saying that I didn't have the potential to go after a professional career and that I should maybe look at going to vocational school.

So I started smoking pot and hanging out like I was expected to do. I graduated from high school in May and married this kid in the neighborhood whom I had known all my life. I did what I was expected to do. I would now live happily ever after and have tons of kids. That's the way it was.

Of course, it didn't work out that way. We were married about two years when I became pregnant. He left me then, and I realized I had a child to raise so I started working full-time. My daughter was born in December, and I continued to work full-time, sometimes two jobs, just trying to make ends meet. At age twenty-seven, I'd had enough of the boring, dull, dead-end jobs, and enrolled at Bemidji State. I chose a variety of courses and discovered I liked criminal justice and social studies. In 1982 I got an undergraduate degree in criminal justice.

I applied to several law schools and was accepted. But at that time, my daughter was starting puberty. I figured law school and puberty were not a good mix! I regrouped and went to Plan B. All I needed to be a police officer in Minnesota was an eight-week skill course. I enrolled in Hibbing Technical College and became one of the first Indian law-enforcement officers in the state. I was scooped up by the Department of Natural Resources and became Minnesota's first female Indian game warden. Looking back, I think I was thrown to the wolves for a few years, sacrificed.

Being a game warden out of Itasca Park was interesting because it was my old home ground, where my family lived, and I was sometimes arresting and giving tickets to my own relatives from the reservation. This was not a real popular thing! There would often be heated arguments. I ended up having to visit my mom at odd hours.

But it wasn't so much the family issues that made me leave. It was the direct sexual harassment I had to deal with as the only woman in this job in northern Minnesota. It was bizarre. I got tired of putting on the armor and going to work every day. So I got a job in a re-entry program in Minneapolis/St. Paul, helping people who had been incarcerated for twenty years or more come back into society. I worked there for about two years and lived in St. Paul. My daughter was fourteen at that time and running wild in the Cities. I had a home north of Bemidji, and I needed to get her out of the metro, so I took a job as director of Indian student services for three community colleges in the Clearwater Community College region.

My daughter screamed while she was in the Cities because she wanted to live back in Bemidji. Then when we moved back to Bemidji, she screamed because she wanted to be back in the metro. This is the hell-child whom I love dearly and who has developed into a wonderful woman. At one time, I worked three jobs in order to maintain our life in St. Paul, keep our home north of Bemidji, and put food on the table and heat in the stove. No wonder she was a wild child. Where the hell was I? Working. Now she's in a med-tech program and has a daughter, my wonderful granddaughter, who is six.

Things didn't improve much when we got back to Bemidji. My job required travel, and I got married again, when my daughter was fifteen. She was outspoken, didn't take any crap from anybody. Then I bring in this guy who is going to set the rules for everyone. What a challenge! In 1986 I entered the master's program at the University of North Dakota. I worked there for about four years and was accepted to a Ph.D. program in counseling psychology in 1993.

What motivated me? What made me pursue this educational path? Through the whole process and basically through my whole adult life, my biggest motivator has been my kids, my daughter and my granddaughter. Without them I wouldn't be who I am today, as independent and strong. My daughter painted me into the corner many times, where I had to say, "Enough!" I was forced to make decisions, like getting my daughter help when she needed it.

The older I get, the more I realize I was isolated from my mother. One day we were sitting around at one of those sisters' weekends, talking about my mom and the relationships that my sisters and I had with her. One of my sisters said, "You know, I just miss her hugging and holding me." I started to think, and I remember saying that I couldn't recall her ever holding me. I can't remember her being affectionate to me, ever. My sisters looked at me like I was some kind of strange duck. Then my older sister said, "Well, I was kind of your mom. I took care of you all the time."

My mom did a lot of things that were wonderful. She was independent, and maybe through observation, I learned some of that. But to sit down and talk? I remember one serious discussion with my mother, after she had her triple bypass when she was seventy years old. We were walking and talking. I had a heart-to-heart with her, the only one I can remember. But, yes, I learned independence growing up in my home.

My mom was always the disciplinarian. My dad was kind of the jolly guy. Mom cracked the whip. Dad was the one we would go to to kiss the boo-boos. He would laugh and joke around with us. But mom made the rules. Don't even question her, because you'd get it. That's the way it was. I can't remember anything we did as kids that was really bad; but on those rare times when we did do something, we had to go out to the lilac bush and cut our own switch. Sometimes we'd get spankings with the wooden spoon. My mom was raised in the Catholic mission schools, like many Indian moms were, where her discipline models were nuns. So what do you expect?

The Catholic church was a big part of our lives growing up. It was something we didn't squawk about. We went to church as a family, and we sat still. Mom had this hatpin. I don't remember being pricked, but she would show it to us: pay attention or you'll get the hatpin.

I'm sort of a pseudo-Catholic. I was married in the church the first time around. Then he left me, when I was three months pregnant. When I went to get the baby baptized, the priest was reluctant to baptize her because her father wasn't involved. And I said, "Look, this kid was conceived in the church!" So then I got a little skeptical about the church and its beliefs. I remember going to church with my mom one Sunday and sitting there with this new baby. The priest was talking about a wife's responsibility, and here was this jerk I was married to, off doing his thing. Who knew where he was? And here I am with the responsibility of this child. I just lost it! I had to get up in the middle of the gospel and leave. My mom was flabbergasted.

Shortly after that, I filed for divorce, another big taboo. Scarlet Letter! Divorcee! I was the first one in my family to be divorced. My sisters were in difficult relationships, but they stuck it out. They stayed married because the church said, "Til death do you part." But I chose not to do that.

The politics of the tribes and reservations cause a lot of problems. For example, because of his birth date, my little brother cannot be enrolled as a tribal member, but he has ten brothers and sisters who are. Think about that. It's ridiculous! Would this happen with the Germans, the Italians, the Swedish, or the Norwegians? What is being Indian? Is it to wear feathers and earrings, or is it to participate in powwows? Is it practicing traditional Indian values? Is it about having a certain amount of Indian blood in your heritage, like full-blood, half-blood, or quarter-blood? The reservations vary on these questions. I'm still trying to sort it out, but it's hard. A very wonderful book called *Night Flying Woman* tells the story of a young Indian woman who finds her identity on the White Earth Reservation. It describes her entire life, from childhood through old age, and finally it tells how the reservation was broken apart. I am still learning about who I am. I guess I always will be.

Ellen (Ellie Mae) Robinson
Born: September 17, 1935

Ellen Robinson lives in a house that stands just fifty feet from the place where she was born. She worked for many years as a gardener at a plant nursery in Park Rapids. While working for Minnesota CEP [Concentrated Employment Program], she became interested in chemical dependency; in 1989 she received her International Consortium Reciprocity Certification, after completing a thirteen-month program at the Hazelden Foundation in Center City, Minnesota. Ellen enjoys her home, her gardens, her relatives, and her dogs. She appreciates living in the home place and often wonders about the history of her people, as well as their future.

Our family lived in a tarpaper shack, and it was cold. But it was our home. We were very poor, but Dad always had a lot of meat on the table because he was a good hunter. After the Depression, he and my brothers built the house that I am living in now. I've been walking these grounds all my life. I left for about eighteen years, while I went to school at Haskell in Kansas, and lived and worked in Minneapolis and Park Rapids. I'm glad to be back where I started.

I attended the Indian boarding school in Kansas because it had been really hard for me in the Mahnomen High School. There were real prejudices back then, and I felt very separate from the rest of the kids. I went through the freshman and sophomore years, and then a couple of my friends and I decided to go to an Indian school. Five of us in my family graduated from Haskell. It was a big school, and I was really unhappy at first. There were Indians from 120 tribes at Haskell then, attending either high school or post–high school. I was taking a prenursing course, but I didn't like it very much. I was very lonely, even physically sick. But they kept us busy, and after a couple of weeks, I was okay.

When I graduated, I went to the Cities and worked various part-time jobs: candy girl at the Gopher Theater, a job at the University of Minnesota, a nurse's aide in St. Paul; I also worked at Honeywell for about three years. Then I spent about a year in Tacoma, Washington, doing odd jobs and baby-sitting for my brother's kids.

When I returned to the Park Rapids area, I got married for the first time. I worked in a nursery there and liked the work. It is a pretty area, and I loved to work with the baby pine trees and have picnics outside on the grounds each day with my coworkers. I met a lot of Finnish women, who showed me how to bake Finn bread. They told me about their saunas, which reminded me a lot of our sweat lodges.

When I was young, my grandpa used to have a home very close to where I live now. He had his own sweat lodge. He would go in there and then come out and jump right in the creek. When he was in the lodge praying, we would sit outside and listen to him chanting and singing. Everything was in the Ojibwe language. He would also tell us stories. He used to eat fish heads. He would boil them, take them apart, and choose the bones to tell us stories about. All the fish bones were shaped like different tools. He would tell us about Wenabozho, which means *creator,* and show us all his tools. He would line them up and tell us fascinating stories.

My mother was married to a man from Wisconsin; he was Ojibwe also but from a different band. Like my grandpa, Mom used to tell us stories about a long time ago and how they used to fight the Sioux. They were enemies in those days. She also taught us a lot about the medicines they used. I still use them.

When I was married to my second husband, I learned a lot from my old mother-in-law. She tried to teach me how to speak Ojibwe, but I never really learned. I think that unless you have someone to practice with, you will never become proficient. I would like to speak the language, but I didn't have enough background because we were discouraged from using it in school.

Certification to work as a chemical-dependency counselor was very difficult because I had to decide how to relate to clients—as a Native American or just as a counselor. There are different ways of approaching problems in each area. It is easier now because Native Americans have their own certification board. When I was certified, that was not available. The board in St. Paul used to be all white people; there weren't any Native Americans on it at that time. Now the different tribes have gotten together and formed their own board, a separate one. I was on the board, helping them make up the questions for the test. They have some tough law-review questions. It isn't easy.

I never care to generalize about chemical dependency when people ask me about my job. Every person I work with is a unique individual. You can't relate to everybody the same. There are a thousand different ways, maybe a million different ways to help people. For instance, some people don't like to be in "group." I learned group work in Hazelden, and it was a confrontational style. That doesn't work well with our people because they are very sensitive from having gone through so much in their lives. They have been so intimidated, and you certainly don't want to add to that. You need to make them feel relaxed and understand that you are the same as they are. And we *are* just the same; there is no difference. They need to feel comfortable with you. Sometimes this takes a long time, but eventually they relate to you.

This process is hard to explain. It's almost like an anointing. Sometimes there isn't anything you can say to a client. All you can do is just be who you are, be there, and be an example. That's a message in itself. It's best not to worry about what you are going to say, but instead just be fully present, with your whole attention on the client.

One thing about our people is they really like to sit and visit and have something funny to laugh at. They all seem to have a terrific sense of humor. They make me laugh all the time. I think I get more out of them than they get out of me. I enjoy working with them.

I have a lot of other interests besides my work. I am a master gardener. I also preserve the plants from my garden, make salsa, pickles, hot sauce, and I can a lot of deer meat. I know a thirteen-year-old hunter who gets me a deer every year. I have three freezers, where I freeze fish and deer meat. I like to eat a lot of wild rice. In the winter, I sew, do puzzles, and help out at the Episcopal church, straight up the hill and one block over. I love to go into that beautiful log church. There is a picture of Jesus on the window with beadwork all around him. It is gorgeous!

I still make baskets when I have the fresh splint, which you make from a black-ash log you find in the woods. It is a long process of cutting, scraping, pounding, and preparing the splint. When that is done, the wood must be soaked, dyed, and hung to dry. When you have made your basket, you cover up the seams with the inner bark of a basswood tree. It's something like raffia. Finally you put sweet grass around the top for decoration and fragrance. My mother taught me how to do this. I hope to get back into basketry after I retire and have more time.

That is what I do with my life, how I keep my days full. I believe that my main responsibility is to take care of myself, to keep myself healthy so that I have good thoughts and a positive attitude to pass on to others. If you feel good and feel happy about yourself, you pass it on to those you meet during your day.

Ellen (Ellie Mae) Robinson

I don't have any children of my own, but I have a lot of nieces, nephews, grandnieces, and grandnephews. And then I have my "wiener" dogs. I don't buy them; they just seem to come to me. People know I like them, and if they see any stray ones around town, they bring them over. They always end up around here.

Sometimes I think about how things have changed in my lifetime. There are so many people now. I remember that when I was small there were trails everywhere, leading to Grandpa's or the neighbors or wherever. People were scattered here and there. It was my job to watch for company, to see if anybody was coming down the trail. Ma would tell me to watch so she could get some lunch ready. The first thing you did when people visited was sit down and have tea and a bite of food, whatever we had on hand. Sometimes it was just bread. So Ma made me the announcer because I had the loudest voice and could run to her and say, "Here comes so-and-so!"

I think the old hospitality is gone. When we saw somebody coming down the trail to visit, it was an honor. People were so glad to see one another. They would hug each other. I will always remember those old ladies, how glad they used to be to see each other, how they would laugh and joke and tell stories. I think we lost a lot when we put people right next door to one another. We need our privacy to appreciate each other.

Elizabeth Foster-Anderson is the controller and accounting manager for the White Earth Indian Reservation's Shooting Star Casino in Mahnomen, Minnesota. After completing a two-year accounting program at Northwest Technical College in Detroit Lakes, she graduated from Moorhead State University in 1989 with a bachelor of arts degree in business administration and a bachelor of science in accounting. Before joining the staff at Shooting Star, she worked for a five-state retail chain and a regional accounting firm, both in Fargo, North Dakota. Elizabeth lives near Detroit Lakes, with her husband and two children.

Elizabeth Foster-Anderson
Born: March 24, 1955

Elizabeth Foster-Anderson

Knowing the history of the Native American working people, I've always wanted to make a difference for them. I want to try to help others—help them get employment, keep their jobs, understand what a payroll check is all about, and maybe get into the idea of budgeting and being self-supporting. That's why I accepted the job of controller and accounting manager for the Shooting Star Casino. It seemed to be the avenue for accomplishing things that were important to me.

This was a start-up operation. Policies and procedures had to be developed, processes had to be set up, and people had to be trained. I liked the objectives behind the casino: to give Indians preference in hiring and to give them work training and the ability to go on and get other jobs and further education. It was meant to be a stepping-stone. That seemed a better objective for me than working for a large corporation, with all the stress and lack of motivation that would involve. The casino is owned and operated by the White Earth Indian Reservation. Every day is a challenge. It's enormous: we employ about a thousand people who all need to be educated, trained, and taught the work ethic. So you can't really compare us with another large company that might have the same number of employees. We are at a different level. We have to work a little bit harder just to reach those objectives and still maintain a for-profit situation. Our profits mean education, employment, and training for the people of White Earth.

Gaming is only one part of Shooting Star. We have a hotel with 250 rooms. We have a conference center with four or five conference rooms for banquets, meetings, and special events. We have a cabaret-entertainment facility that showcases big-name country entertainment. We have three restaurants—one that's gourmet style, a buffet that seats 350 people, and a coffee shop that seats 180. We are a twenty-four-hour operation, so it keeps us going, seven days a week. Nothing ever stops. We're always busy.

My father, James McDougall Foster, is a native of White Earth. He was put through college by a grant from an Indian educational program and graduated with a degree in engineering. His work took our family all over the United States.

After he retired, he settled back in Minnesota near his homeland. So I moved back to this area with my family when I was fourteen.

When I was eighteen, after many years of teenage trial and error, I became the mother of a wonderful son, Christopher. I had a responsibility for him that I wasn't ready for. However, my father and my mother gave me values; I realized I couldn't spend my life on welfare, and I had the drive to make a difference. I knew that being a single mother on welfare was not the life I wanted for Christopher or me.

Just out of high school, I went into a two-year accounting program at the vocational college in Detroit Lakes. When I graduated, I realized right away that it wasn't enough education to get me to the goals and accomplishments I had in mind for myself. So I went directly to Moorhead State University to obtain a bachelor of arts degree in business administration and a bachelor of science in accounting. I spent several years as a tax accountant and was controller for a retail store for a five-state area. I worked for a regional accounting firm for several years as an auditor. Then I went to work for the Shooting Star Casino on November 21, 1991, the day it opened.

When you talk about the casino, you're not just talking about making sure we have a growing concern that's going to be there for the rest of our lives. You're talking about trying to change a cycle that has existed for years and years, even for centuries. That's the way I look at it every day when I go to work. There are times when it's very difficult and you're working fourteen, sixteen, eighteen hours a day. I hang onto the fact that we are here to accomplish something, to make a difference. It can be a big job.

Since Congress passed the Self-Determination Act in 1975, the Indian tribal leaders have been trying to put things into place that will change the cycle. It's been a tough road for them. When you look back on the history of the White Earth Indian Reservation, not a lot of businesses that it owns are profitable. This is the key to changing that. With profits from the casino, they can improve their education programs, improve their employment and training programs, and improve some of their social-welfare programs. They believe they'll be able to accomplish that.

With any political organization comes conflict. The White Earth Indian Reservation is a federally recognized government, so you see it here, too. Some people do not support us out there. If you compare our politics to those of local government, it is no different. When construction began on a fifteen-million-dollar gaming complex back in 1991, there were dissidents who didn't think a casino was the answer for the White Earth Indian Reservation. I have talked to a few of them, and I recognize some of their reasoning. But I'll tell you, for the past couple of years a lot of the dissidents who took part in protests and sit-ins in 1991 are no longer dissidents. They work for the Shooting Star Casino.

If you talk to a good handful of the people, you'll find they are all working toward the same objectives. Tribal leaders planned this business to bring self-determination to the reservation. They took the risk and weighed the controversy against the long-term objectives they wanted to gain: decreasing poverty, increasing the work ethic, decreasing unemployment on the reservation, and providing a stepping-stone for Indian people.

I think the White Earth Indian Reservation has made one of the better decisions in its history as far as establishing the casino for economic development. If I had to compare our operation with those on other Indian reservations on a scale of zero to ten, I'd say White Earth runs at an eight. We have good people here, and they work hard to get what they want.

When you bring in gambling, you're bringing in what everyone would identify as a black cloud. Nevada legalized gaming more than fifty years ago, during the era of Prohibition, when mobsters ran black markets. That stigma has stayed with the industry ever since. The biggest fear of opponents to gambling is that organized crime will come in and assume that reservation people are illiterate or uneducated and that they can be easily manipulated. When I first came into the business, organized crime was one of my own concerns as well, but not now. At the Shooting Star, I do not see that. Our activities are regulated by powerful organizations, such as the Minnesota Department of Public Safety and the National Indian Gaming Association.

The White Earth Tribal Council is responsible for operating the Shooting Star Casino, along with all other reservation businesses. They hired a management company in 1991 that had expertise in gaming; the company reported to the council for four and a half years, until August 12, 1996. From the beginning, the council's objective has been to run this as a family-entertainment and gaming complex. They want to project the image of entertainment, and they advised all their department heads that this was the objective. They do not want to encourage addictive gambling.

The management company's primary objective was to train Indian personnel to run the operation in the future. About fourteen of the twenty department managers are enrolled members who were trained to take over at the end of the contract. That objective has been accomplished—not because of previous tribal leaders or the management company but because the people themselves accomplished it. They've had the will to make a difference. They've built a successful operation that future generations will benefit from.

Events in 1996 have changed the reservation for the better. Corrupt tribal leaders were indicted for their activities at the tribal headquarters. The Indian people assessed their tribal leadership and wanted change. It came in June, when a new government was formed. After many years of oppression under the old leadership, new voices are finally being heard.

Since we moved back to this area, my father has taken me to every powwow that's been held. I take my children to some of the Indian cultural events on the reservation. I want them to see their culture and get a good idea of what it means to be a real Indian—and not just the stereotype.

My philosophy is that I am a person who is not different because I'm Indian, black, white, or Hispanic. My children carry a lot of my own strong feelings with them. We are all individuals with our own abilities, and we all can accomplish things in our lives.

Leigh Harper
Born: June 22, 1981

Leigh Harper is a fourteen-year-old student at Park Rapids High School. A quiet, serious girl, she is recognized at school as an accomplished artist and a good student. Leigh is considering a possible career as a doctor. She lives with her parents, two of her three brothers, and her younger sister near Pine Point on the White Earth Reservation.

I visit my grandmother and grandfather every day. They live about a mile from our home, on the edge of the projects. My grandmother is like a second mother to me, my brothers and sister, and some of my cousins. She baby-sits my baby brother when my mom is working. My grandfather had a stroke, and I see him daily just to see how he is doing. I usually get off the school bus near there and stay with them until my mom gets off work, anything from a half-hour to three or four hours. Once a week or so, I'll cook something for them, like peanut-butter cookies, cakes from scratch, or pies.

My grandparents are very tolerant. They let us get away with more stuff. They do the small things that really matter, like baking me something or maybe helping me on something I can't understand. On occasion my grandmother tells about something that happened in her childhood, like how her family was always moving to different places.

My mother is like a best friend to me. I can talk easily to her. She always listens, but she can draw the line. When I step out of line, she'll punish me for stuff. I've learned not to do that. She has rules and she'll enforce them, usually by talking to us in a stricter voice. Our parents tell us kids where we went wrong and then see if we understand it. They might cut our allowance, or if we've done something really bad, we might be grounded for weeks. They always have the last word. But they let us know they love us and are proud of us. Their approval means a lot to us.

I have an Arabian horse named Ibbon, and my sister has two Shetland ponies, Dusty and Jewel. We saved up our money over the years and paid for them ourselves. One of my chores is feeding all the animals—the horses, our three dogs, a cat, and a fish. I also take care of animals at my grandmother's house. She has two dogs and my cat there.

We go see my grandparents on my father's side up at Cass Lake once a month or so. My aunt and two of my cousins live with them, along with my grandmother's adopted daughter, who's ten now. I spend a lot of time with my cousins. Everyone in the community is related to me in some way.

I'm saving up my money to buy a car when I get my license. I clean houses for other people sometimes, and they pay me for that. Sometimes I do folding at a dry cleaners. My mom gives me an allowance every week, and I've gotten some money from art contests that I've entered.

I've been interested in art ever since I was a little girl. I'd draw on the backs of books and on the walls with crayons. Mom would get really mad. Now the walls are painted over, so there are no more marks left.

I started entering drawing contests when I was in middle school. Somebody would just give me a piece of paper about the contest, and I would enter. My entry in a natural-resources poster contest through school made it to the state level; that was in fourth grade, I think. There have been other contests, too. Some I've won. I won second place in the "Don't Use Drugs" contest in sixth grade, and then won first place the next year.

Most recently I was in an international contest called "Peace in My World," which was sponsored by the Lions Club. From what I know, I made it past state and part of Canada, up to New York, where mine was in the top seventy-five posters. I think a girl from Turkey won the top prize.

At school everyone wants me to draw them something. I think I'm really good at drawing horses. I've been drawing them since I was a little girl. I study a lot. I took algebra in eighth grade in a special class. I'm in geometry now. Numbers always have come easy to me. And science is fun. I've thought about being a doctor. My mom would really like that.

I'm usually reading all the time. I can read a five-hundred-page book in two days if I don't have anything else to do. It started when my dad gave me a Stephen King book to read while we were in Canada for the Native American Olympics, which I took part in. I just started reading then. I buy books from the book clubs in magazines. I've enjoyed the *Star Wars* books from the Science Fiction Book Club.

I ride the school bus to and from Park Rapids about an hour a day, and I use that time to read. Some of the kids on the bus can get pretty rowdy, but I block them out when I'm reading. I've developed a tendency to ignore people when I'm in a book. Sometimes my mother will have to call my name two or three times before I hear her.

My grandparents both have a high quantum of Indian blood, so my heritage is important to me. I enjoy listening to them talk about it. It probably means more to me now than when I was younger. I've always enjoyed being Indian because it is unique, more unique than white or Mexican-American. To me it means that I might be stronger spiritually.

I have Indian friends and white friends at school. There's a small number of kids in school who call people names and tease them, but I usually just let it roll off my back and ignore them. My mother has always said not to feel put down if people tease me about my heritage, because it's special.

Most of the time I feel pretty content and comfortable with myself, but I do fall into moods where I am sad for no reason. That probably only lasts for half an hour. I seem to like being alone. Maybe it comes from being around isolated places. Around here we are mainly out in the country, away from people. On the other hand, most of the people in school know me, and I do have friends in every class I can relate to, both whites and Indians.

Beverly Warren

Born: October 10, 1956

Beverly Warren is codirector of the Northwoods Coalition for Battered Women in Bemidji, Minnesota. She has served on and chaired many local, state, and national committees and boards, including the American Indian Women's Circle against Abuse, Battered Women's Advisory Council, the Minnesota Coalition for Battered Women, the Racial Bias Task Force in Bemidji, and the Ninth Judicial District Domestic Violence Team. Born on the White Earth Reservation, she graduated from Waubun High School and has attended Rochester Community College and Mankato and Bemidji State Universities. She lives with her partner and their two teen-age children in Bemidji.

Some people move to the city and never come back. Some people go to the city and continue to come back to the res. Some people are real traditional; they stay at the res and don't ever go anywhere. I feel like I'm kind of in the middle. Even though I live in Bemidji, my coworker tells me, "You go to the reservation like I go to the grocery store." If there's a birthday during the week and I can make it, I'll drive over here. I visit my parents almost every weekend. I'm here a lot.

There are six kids in my family, and I am the middle daughter. We're a close-knit family, but we are not a quiet one. We all talk. When we get together, you know we are there. Actually, that's where a lot of my strength comes from, from my family. I spend a lot of time with them. My family and I have just great fun!

I've always been interested in women and in choice. The Northwoods Coalition for Battered Women deals with both topics. At the shelter, it has been wide open for me to build on what I like, what I want to do, and where I want to go.

For me, the bottom line is that if someone hits you, it hurts. It doesn't matter who you are or what color you are. One of the things you find with domestic violence in families is that it covers all racial lines, income levels, classes, and religions.

One of the harder things in working with violence among Native Americans is that it is such a close-knit community. Confidentiality is real hard. How do you keep someone safe when everyone knows who you are and where you are? We work really hard in our program to maintain confidentiality.

I wanted our shelter to operate an Indian program on the reservation so that our women wouldn't have to leave to get help. I feel that Native American families often want to keep their problems in the family: "You don't need to get help out there; you don't need to talk to those people; just stay here."

Violence is never okay. It's not okay to be violent, whether you are a boy or a girl. It's not okay to be mentally abusive. I try to work toward those kinds of things. I don't have any quick fixes. My only one would be to deal with the children early on in families where there is violence.

When I first came over here [to the reservation], one of the things I thought would help abused women was to strengthen their spirituality. I brought people in to talk in depth on questions like "What is my role as a woman?" and "What is my role as a Native American woman?" and on the whole culture and its history. I want women to have knowledge about being Native American and about our culture. I want women to be given the knowledge because, to me, knowledge is power.

As I've gotten older, I've realized that a lot of Native Americans do not know their culture or traditions or history. I want women to know their history and to feel their strength. Women within the Indian culture are the caregivers and have the babies. To me, that is a big strength. I try to talk to women about that strength—that we are the strong ones. We are the ones who keep the families together. I want women to feel good about that strength.

We do have roles as women. As a woman, if I go into a ceremony, I'm supposed to do certain things, wear a skirt and act a certain way, and I'm fine with that. But when I come back out into the community, I have choices, and I make those choices as an individual.

During the boarding-school era, Indian children were taken from their homes, period. They didn't have a choice. They were put into the boarding-school system to take away their culture and their traditions.

Indian history was oral history; it was not written in books. Grandparents and uncles and aunts taught it to children. Part of Ojibwe culture was that the parents would raise the children, and the children would learn from the parents how to raise their children.

My grandmother was taken out of the home and put into a boarding school as a child. She always dyed her hair a platinum blond. I never even knew she spoke Indian until I was twenty-two years old, not until I lived with her one summer. She started singing Indian songs, and I said, "Grandmother, I never knew you knew how to sing."

She said, "It was never a good thing to know."

I said, "I never knew you knew how to speak Indian. Why didn't you teach me?"

She said, "My girl, I thought it was best for me *not* to teach you."

Our struggle has always been different. I think our struggle is to remain who we are—to keep our culture and traditions. I try to teach my children this. When I talk to people of any race, I find it's the same struggle: to maintain who you are.

I think prejudice is a lot less blatant now, but it's more insidious. You can feel it. It's there, even if they are not calling you a dumb Indian. The undercurrents are still there. Some days, it's great. Other days, it's a real pain in the butt.

That's such a hard subject to talk about. In my family, for instance, my younger sister, Debra, has blue eyes, brown hair, and light skin. I'm the middle one. I look more Indian; I'm a little darker skinned and have brown eyes. My older sister, Terri, has almost black hair, dark skin, and dark eyes. She definitely looks like an Indian. The reality is that we all have the same mother and father, we're all Indian, we're all enrolled, we're all from White Earth, we've all lived here.

Debra is treated like a white person by Indians because she has light skin, light hair, and light eyes. Yet she still feels prejudice from white people because they know where she's from. I, on the other hand, will feel race and prejudice a lot more from white people, but Indians are more accepting of me because I go to ceremonies, and I dance, and I'm out in the community. Terri feels it very much from the white community. She lives on the res and always has. She has a reservation license right on her car. She's gone to Fargo and people have given her the finger straight out. They have screamed out, "Go back to where you came from."

It's just such a different reality for each of us. We are all from the same family, but look different. It's like the darker you are, the more you're going to feel it. I think that my sister who is the lightest feels prejudice as a double-edged sword, because some Native Americans don't really like her because she is too light, and some white people don't like her because she is an Indian.

Even though I lived on the reservation until I was seventeen, I had to leave it in order to find my culture. Spirituality has always been in my life. When I was at home, it was Catholic. When I left home, I was still seriously searching for my spirituality. At that point, I met my partner. I was eighteen. We were looking for the same thing. We both started going to ceremonies and to sweats together. When I went into a sweat or into a ceremony, it reached into the nuts and bolts of me. It no longer had to do with anybody else in the room but me. I feel like my spirituality has made me strong.

Native American spirituality is less structured. When we go to powwows, we camp with people. We share food together and talk together. We don't always have a ceremony, but to me, it feels spiritual. I'm out there in my dress with my long hair.

I've had long hair now for probably twenty years. My mother says, "You're turning forty. Why do you have long hair?" I say, "Mom, I'm probably always going to have long hair. It's part of my strength and who I am."

I do antiracism work because I think it's important that people see and hear and understand about the good things—teaching our children about our culture, feeling our spirituality, coming into a ceremony or a give-away, seeing us just being families. That's the positive part of who I am. You are never going to know what an Indian person feels like, the whole reality of it, if you are not one.

I want to expose people to the positives. They get such a thick layer of the negative, between radio and TV and newspapers. I want them to get a sense of the positive role models and all the positive things that are happening among us.

Frances Keahna was born more than ninety years ago on a farm in Heier Township, northwest of Mahnomen on the White Earth Reservation. Her Ojibwe name was Nenaakowabikwe. Noted for her mastery of traditional Chippewa basket making, she demonstrated her art and exhibited her baskets at the Minnesota State Fair, the Minnesota State Historical Society, and many other locations, and she worked with the Minnesota State Arts Council. Mrs. Keahna, who lost her husband of forty years in 1965, was the mother of six daughters and one son. She was well known and respected throughout the reservation as an elder with a wonderful sense of humor.

Frances Keahna

Born: March 25, 1905
Died: February 15, 1998

I'm the last Goodwin. They're all gone—my mother, my father, my grandmother, my brother, and my two sisters. I was the second to the youngest, and now I'm the only one left.

We lived on a little farm in Heier Township near Duelm. Everybody had certain jobs. We all pitched in and did things together, like feeding the chickens, slopping the hogs, and feeding and watering the horses and the cattle.

We had to make a lot of our own food in those days. We had our own gardens and did a lot of canning. We'd go pick berries and can them or make jellies and jams. We raised our own meat right on the farm, and pumped water from a little creek down the hill from our place. My mother made dried sweet corn. She'd buy a whole bunch of corn, cut it off the cob, lay it on cheesecloth, and put it out on racks. I've never made it myself, but I did like to eat it!

We got around with horses and buggies. Every morning we milked the cows and separated the milk with an old-fashioned separator before we walked to school, about a quarter mile away. I remember making our own trails through the deep snow. We had a store, a church, a post office, and the school in those days. Now it's all fields. Everything is gone.

Our first school had one room with all the grades from first through eighth. We brought sandwiches for lunch in a little syrup pail. We studied the ABCs, math, and just the everyday language. Of course, it was easier in those days, not like it is today. We had a strict old man for a teacher who'd hit you with a ruler. Nowadays that would be abuse!

My mother's father was a Warren. Her great-grandfather, William W. Warren, wrote the book *The History of the Ojibway People*. My grandmother was a Chippewa—from Canada, I think.

My father's father, old George Goodwin, was white. He came from Maine, over the Great Lakes with the fur traders and trappers. My grandmother spoke Ojibwe, but she didn't speak English very well. My father and mother never spoke Ojibwe unless there was something they didn't want us to know, so I never learned the language outside of a few basic words. I don't recall them ever discouraging us from using it, though.

We lived on the farm until 1918, when my father ran out of work. He was a logger, and used to drive logs down the Rice River. When work ran out, we moved here to Nay-tah-waush. He became a carpenter and built a lot of these houses around here.

I went to school here through eighth grade. After about a half year of high school, I transferred to the Haskell Institute, an Indian boarding school at Lawrence, Kansas. I was there for about three years. I don't think I came home at all, except for the summers. Of course, I never did stay on the campus. I had a job. I took care of some elders and stayed right in their home.

I met my husband in school. He was a football player—and you know how that goes! They were winning all the games. He was from Iowa, a Sac and Fox Indian. We Chippewa liked to chase the Sac and Fox down! We were married February 17, 1925, in Toledo, Ohio. He died in 1965. I've never remarried, and I haven't been looking. There's nobody around who could keep up with me anyway, even if I am ninety years old. My son-in-law calls me the ringleader.

I have seven children, all living. My daughter Deanna lives in Burnsville. In her house, she has every kind of basket I've ever made—baskets all over. She and her husband are retired from the BIA [Bureau of Indian Affairs]. One daughter lives in Oklahoma now. She used to live in Chicago, but she had little tots growing up. They would come home all beat up, so she said, "That's enough." She works with records in a hospital there. Nancy is in Idabelle, Oklahoma. Bonnie's in Dallas. Cookie's in San Mateo, California. Vincent is in Minneapolis; he's retired from the BIA, too. And Lauren works here at the school in Nay-tah-waush.

I can't remember exactly when I started making baskets. It's so long ago! My mother learned basket making through an Episcopal minister who came here to our church. They were Ottawa Chippewas from way up on the peninsula of Michigan. His mother came here to visit, and she taught my mother basket making. My mother didn't stick with it because it was such hard work, but she taught me how to do it.

I've often given demonstrations of my basket making at craft shows and exhibits. I've been to the Minnesota State Fair three times. I've been down at

Chanhassen. I've been all along the Iron Range. We once went over to a show at Cass Lake with a big bundle of about twenty-five baskets. We started out at ten in the morning, and by two o'clock, we had only one basket left. The others still had their baskets. It wasn't the price, either. I asked a woman I know who's a coordinator for the aging if she wanted to buy it. She said, "Sure, I'll buy it." And we went home with nothing left.

I've worked with the State Arts Board and have been to the Historical Society in St. Paul and all over the city. I went to the tribal college in Cass Lake last April and to Maplewood State Park in May. They wanted me at some other events, but enough is enough. I said, "I'm getting too old for this." But making baskets does make me feel good.

Up until 1966, I set [fishing] nets through the ice. We went ricing and sugar bushing. Our family would tap hundreds of trees right up the road, four or five miles north of the village. It would take three good weeks. We made sugar cake and syrup to keep through the winter. It took a lot of boiling of the sap to get the syrup. Nowadays they are really making it easier and better with the evaporators and plastic tubes, but we did it all the hard way.

I learned a lot about using medicinal plants from my mother. We'd go out and pick the plants in the fall after they had blossomed. I remember picking pennyroyal; you make a hot tea from it to use for cold or congestion. It would make you sweat and bring the cold right out of you.

For headaches you can use parts of the birch tree—the little shelves, the fungus things that grow on their white bark. You take off the shell and remove the brown part on the inside, then burn a piece about the size of your fingernail in an ashtray. Cover your head with a towel and inhale the smoke, and your headache is gone. I still use that when I get a headache. You just try it! You have to believe in it, though—believe that it's going to get you well.

Once I talked to a medicine man from Montana. I told him I have tendonitis in my shoulders. I gave him some tobacco, and he sent his helper out to the car to bring back some medicine, a little bottle full of greaselike stuff that came from a female bear. I rubbed just a little of it on my shoulders. Before I saw him, I couldn't move my arms. Now I can raise them.

I'm satisfied with things just the way they are now. I'm not hard to please. I watch TV, read, work puzzles, and make baskets when I feel like it. And I like to play bingo. One Sunday morning, I went to play bingo. They feed you a free dinner, then you have all afternoon and night to play, so I stayed all day. That night when I got home, I saw numbers everywhere I looked. Numbers on the doorknobs. Numbers all over the place. I thought I was going crazy! But I'm still healthy. See, I don't have arthritis, and I don't have diabetes. But I do have bingo eyes!

Vance Vannote is a practicing psychologist in Fargo, North Dakota. He has been an avid student of photography since 1974.